THE POWER OF TWO

By

W. Foster Welborn

Copyright # TX 7-604-973 2012
by W. Foster Welborn

ISBN-13: 978-0615892498

ISBN-10: 0615892493

If you would like to contact me,

My Website is: **www.wfosterwelborn.com** for information, E-mail and feedback on this book.

My Mailing Address is:

PO Box 745865
Arvada, CO 80006-5865

This book is available at:

https://www.createspace.com/4453210

or Amazon.com and also from the Amazon.com Kindle Store under my author name or book title.

To My Wife, Mary Lou,

Who loves my stories,

Encourages and puts up with me.

Look for my other books on Kindle:

The Power of One

The Power of Two

Smoking Earth River

Dah-A-Sah

Autumn Leaves

Look for these books on Nook:

The Power of One

The Power of Two

Look for my other book on
https://www.CreateSpace.com/4009384
and onAmazon.com:

The Power of One

THE POWER OF TWO, BOOK 2 of The Power of One Series:

Table of Contents

CHAPTER 1

Miranda was in the Receiving Room of He Who Summons. She had a premonition concerning the reason her presence had been requested. When He began speaking, she knew her hunch had been right.

"Miranda, I would like you to make a little trip to Earth to bring David and his son, Jonathan, back here. David should update his training anyway. It's time. Jonathan needs a little training as well, before he realizes his power and maybe misapplies it. Of course, he's so very young that you'll probably have to use a much different approach with him. Do you think you can accomplish that?"

She thought about her response before replying with: "A lot will depend on Jonathan and how well he understands his power and its use, and how fast he can absorb the necessary information. I will say that even a small amount of the necessary training is better than no training at all."

He Who Summons smiled and said, "You know, I have been so excited that genetic transfer could take place, and now it has actually occurred in this case!"

"What do I do about Melody? She will, of necessity, have to be informed about David and Jonathan coming here because their biological bodies will still be at home on Earth. She will need to know and understand the healing power and what We are doing. In light of this, how far do You wish me to go?" she asked.

He responded, "That's true enough. I trust your good judgment on how much to divulge. Personally, I think that, if you explain to Melody how David used his knowledge and power to heal her, and you in turn used this same process to heal Jonathan, she will appreciate that what We are doing is only for the good of humanity and will cooperate."

"If Melody agrees with Us, as Jonathan gets older, he could visit Us several times for more training and instruction in certain areas," she replied. "Why not bring her for a visit so she could see our Planet? Then she would truly know that We mean well."

His eyes lit up in actual excitement as He leaned toward Miranda in His chair.

"That is the best idea of all! I don't know why I didn't think of it! Maybe We should bring Melody for a visit first so she can learn about Us. What do you think about that?" He asked.

She replied, "I agree. I'll speak to David about it and enlist his help to convince her to come here. If she agrees, it will be up to Us to let her see Our good intentions. Our next

2

step would be easy—have David and Jonathan come here together." Miranda smiled and continued, "If all goes well, We would have had the whole family here in a very short while."

He Who Summons rose, clapped His hands eagerly, and said, "We have a good plan, and I'd like you to get started on Our little project as soon as possible."

Miranda rose from her chair, laughed, and said, "I'll get on it right away, Master."

CHAPTER 2

School days had begun once more. Jonathan, along with his best friend, Petey, were now in the Third Grade.

Jonathan finished his breakfast in record time and was already moving towards the front door when Melody's voice stopped him in his tracks.

"Where do you think you're going, young man?" she inquired.

"Mom, you know I'm going to school. Is there something wrong?" he asked in return.

"Perhaps you've forgotten something important?" she quizzed.

He looked around the kitchen with a puzzled look on his face.

Finally, he looked at his mom and asked, "What did I miss?"

"Where's your jacket? I see that you've also left your lunch on the counter," she replied.

He retrieved his lunch and shrugged into his jacket as he made his way towards the front door.

"Aren't you forgetting the most important thing of all?" she asked, with a mock look of hurt on her face.

"Aw, Mom," he said as he hurried over to give her a big hug and kiss.

"Now, that's so much better," she smiled at him brightly. "Hurry along now or you'll miss your school bus. Tell Petey hello for me, and give my regards to his Mom, Elsa."

He waved at her and disappeared out the door quickly.

Melody thought, "Jonathan and Petey are such big chums! Usually, when you see one, the other one is there too. They are birds of a feather, just like two peas in a pod. When they aren't in school, we'll find them playing together at our house or Petey's. It's fun to watch them playing and enjoying each other's company. Many times, Elsa and I have wondered just what they're talking about or what scheme they are trying to hatch when they've got their heads together."

She laughed to herself as she went about her morning chores.

Petey and Jonathan were playing during recess at school. Jonathan had thrown a small football towards Petey.

Rodney, who was a much bigger boy and loved to bully smaller boys, yelled, "Get out of the way, you shrimp!" as he roughly shoved Petey to the ground so he could catch the football.

"Hey!" shouted Petey, jumping up. "Give me back that ball! Jonathan and I are playing catch."

Petey tried to jump up and grab the ball back, but Rodney just sneered and pushed Petey down to the ground again, even more roughly.

"You talk real big for such a little shrimp," Rodney stated menacingly.

By this time, Jonathan had run over to Petey, who was still on the ground.

He looked at Rodney and asked him, "Why don't you pick on somebody your own size?"

Rodney put his hand on Jonathan's chest and started pushing hard.

"You mean someone like you, wimp?" he sneered at Jonathan.

Jonathan calmly grabbed Rodney's hand, and the heat began flowing through his touch.

Acute pain flew up Rodney's arm, and he cried out loudly, "Yikes! What are you doing to me? That hurts!"

Rodney thought, "This pain is unlike anything I've ever experienced before!"

Out loud, he said through gritted teeth, "Let me go!"

"Say please," replied Jonathan.

Meanwhile, Petey had regained his feet and was watching Jonathan handle this big bully very calmly.

"Wow!" he thought, as his mouth dropped open in surprise.

Rodney said in the same pain-filled voice, "Please."

Jonathan commanded, "Louder!"

"Please!" Rodney said even louder.

Jonathan eased up a little on the heat, thinking, "This pain is still enough to control this bully!"

Jonathan smiled as he spoke again, "You owe Petey an apology, don't you? Let's hear it!"

Rodney looked at Petey with his eyes still glazed with the pain and said, "I'm sorry for pushing you, Petey."

Jonathan eased up some more on the heat and told Rodney, "You'd better not hurt Petey, me, or anyone else! Next time, I won't be as easy on you as I've been this time!"

Jonathan released his grip on Rodney, looked him in the eyes and said, "Now beat it!"

Rodney took off running without even looking back.

Petey looked at his friend and said, "That was great, Jonathan!"

He responded, "Petey, don't tell anyone about this, OK? Let's keep this just between us. Would you do that for me?"

Petey looked at him, responded with a smile, and said, "After what you just did for me, how could I say no? Don't worry, I won't tell. Come on, we have time to toss the ball a little more before recess is over."

They tossed the ball back and forth.

"Thanks, Petey," said Jonathan. "You're a good buddy."

Jonathan looked at Petey carefully. He could see that he had only gotten a couple of minor scratches out of the scuffle, but nothing serious.

He thought, "He's going to be OK."

The bell sounded, ending recess. The two little friends filed back into their classroom.

CHAPTER 3

Miranda arrived on Earth at David's house, clothed in an Earthling's dress appropriate for the time period, timing her visit so David would be home from work and Jonathan would be playing over at Petey's house, as usual. She rang the door bell.

Melody answered the door.

When she saw Miranda, she did not recognize her, so she asked, "Yes, can I help you?"

Miranda smiled at her and said, "Hello, Melody. You don't know me, but my name is Miranda. Is David at home? I need to speak with the two of you, as a matter of fact."

"He's in the living room," Melody replied as David came up behind her to see who was at the door.

"Actually, I'm right here," he said.

David's face instantly registered a look of astonishment when he saw Miranda.

"Hello, David," Miranda said as she smiled at him over Melody's shoulder. "May I come in? We need to talk."

"Of course, please do," David spoke as Melody stood aside to allow Miranda enough space to enter.

Melody looked at David with a very puzzled look, communicating to him that she was not happy with what was happening with this unknown woman.

David, smiling at their guest, said, "Let's sit and talk in the living room where we can be comfortable. Honey, I've been planning to tell you about Miranda, but since she's here, I'll let her explain everything. I think that might be why she has come. It's probably very different than what you might be thinking. Am I right, Miranda?"

When they were seated, Miranda looked at Melody's unhappy face and smilingly answered, "Yes. In fact, David and I have been acquainted for quite some time."

With that, she began at the beginning to tell the story, leaving nothing out. By the time she had finished, Melody looked so relieved.

Melody thought, "My bafflement and fears have simply disappeared as I listened to the story. It is so amazing!"

Aloud, she said, "Thank goodness! I appreciate your telling me about this. It answers so many questions!"

Miranda responded, "He Who Summons sent me to talk to both of you on behalf of Jonathan. We wish to give him some very basic training about the use of his power before he injures someone unknowingly. After all, he is so very young. We thought that, if Melody would accept an invitation to visit Us on Gorbandihar, she could see that We mean no harm—only good. Hopefully, at that time, she will agree to let you and Jonathan come to my Planet for training."

With that, she hesitated and then laughed as David began talking excitedly.

"Melody, you'll really enjoy Gorbandihar! They are advanced far ahead of us. Why, we actually look primitive in comparison!"

Miranda thought the moment had arrived for a small demonstration.

"Would you please excuse me for a moment?" she asked as she rose and went into the guest bedroom.

Very quickly, Miranda transformed into her flowing gown, golden girdle and sandals. Soon afterward, she returned to the living room.

Melody's jaw dropped as she said, "Oh, how beautiful!"

Miranda smiled as she communicated to Melody with mental telepathy: "This is how I dress on my Planet. This is how we communicate, except not in this language."

Melody nodded that she understood and formed a question in her mind, "Does David know how to do this kind of communication?"

Miranda smiled again as she thought, "No, David just uses your spoken language. You're doing very well for a first try. Thought exchange is much easier and a whole lot faster."

"I think so, too," thought Melody, experiencing a growing sense of excitement.

David quietly watched their faces, knowing they were exchanging thoughts.

Finally, he put his arm around Melody's shoulder and spoke softly, "I've wanted to tell you for a long time, but I didn't know how you would react. I didn't want to upset you. What I'm doing is good, and benefits our people. I can't tell anyone because they are not ready. Besides, they wouldn't believe me anyway. I know that He Who Summons and Miranda can explain it all and show you how it works—it's very difficult knowledge that is made simple for one to absorb and remember. I would like you to go and experience Gorbandihar because then you would be able to understand completely. Besides, Jonathan and I will get by just fine."

He looked at Miranda and asked, "How long in Earth time would Melody need to visit with you and He Who Summons?"

Miranda thought for a few seconds and replied, "Three but no more than four Earth days should do very nicely."

Miranda turned back towards the guest bedroom and spoke over her shoulder, "Please excuse me again."

She went back into that room and quickly transformed back into her Earthling dress. She returned to the living room.

"Wow!" thought Melody. "How marvelous!"

Miranda responded with telepathy, "I'm glad you think that. When you and I travel to Gorbandihar, I believe you'll really like my Planet very much."

Aloud, Melody asked, "When will we leave?"

Miranda responded, "A couple of Earth days should be enough time for you and David to plan. Just tell your friends that you'll be going somewhere for a short visit. You don't have to explain where you're going."

Just then, there was a bang at the front door as Jonathan came in, slamming the door with his foot. He came into the living room.

Upon seeing the beautiful lady, he smiled warmly and said, "Hi!"

"Hello, it's so nice to see you again, Jonathan," she responded. "My, how tall you've grown. My name is Miranda."

Melody looked at Jonathan and said, "How many times have I told you not to slam that door?"

Jonathan was embarrassed and looked down at his feet, shuffling them.

"I'm sorry. I forgot again, Mom," he said.

Melody said, "Go run your bath water, young man. Don't forget to wash your ears."

"Aw, Mom," Jonathan said as he moved towards the bathroom.

David laughed and stated, "He usually loves taking a bath."

Melody laughed, too, and said, "Boys will be boys."

Miranda rose to leave and smiled as she spoke to Melody, "You won't need anything special for the trip. David will explain how it works. I'll be looking forward to seeing you day after tomorrow. It's so good to finally get the opportunity to meet you after all these years. Good evening to both you."

She then rose through the ceiling.

"My goodness!" exclaimed Melody.

David simply laughed and said, "Told you they were advanced!"

After a few moments, Melody looked at David and said, "I knew it was you all along who healed me because I saw you that night!"

She laughed at the surprised look on David's face.

"I woke up and saw you leave," she said, smiling. "I figured it out when you visited me the next day but had to leave my room to go change your clothes so you could leave the hospital. Oh, and by the way, thanks. I appreciate my healing more than you'll ever know! " and then she kissed him soundly.

CHAPTER 4

Bob Michaels woke up with a terrible hangover the day after he struck Julie. He was sorry he had struck her while in a drunken stupor. He soon realized that Julie had left and did not plan to come back because she had taken almost all of her clothes and much of the baby's stuff.

He thought, "She must have really been fed-up with me. She packed up and left at night. I messed up big time with her, and now there's no one to blame but myself! Still, she did not have the right to run away with my son. After all, he's my son, too!"

He did not realize how pathetic his thought really was.

He tracked down many of Julie's college class mates to see if they might know where she had gone. Any of the ones he found either did not know or would not tell him anything. After all, they were familiar with how he had treated her.

He continued working and, of course, drinking. Try as he might, he was unable to break his addiction to alcohol. He was not a jolly drunk either. Instead, he was a mean drunk with a chip on his shoulder. He did not have any friends as people did not want to be around him when he was intoxicated.

He was almost convinced he would never see his wife or son again, but he kept hoping. He had a few relationships with different women, but none of them lasted very long. He had moved several times, changing apartments, but somehow he remembered to use mail forwarding through the Post Office.

Still, it came as a surprise to receive a thick brown envelope postmarked with an Aurora, Colorado, return address. When he opened the envelope and scanned the contents, he found Divorce papers which Julie had sent.

He tapped the envelope and thought, "So that's where she went!"

He smiled to himself.

"Won't she be surprised when I show up on her door step? David will be somewhere close by his mother, but he is still my son, too! A carpenter job in Denver or Aurora should not be hard to find. Everything I own, especially my tools, will fit in my pickup truck. All that I really need now is my paycheck, which I'll get in two more days. There's no sense in getting in a sweat about anything after all these years. Julie and David aren't going anywhere, and neither am I without money. I know I won't recognize David now, nor will he recognize me. When Julie left, he was just a little boy. As a matter of fact, I don't have any idea what I can say when I meet my son, who will be a man now. In fact, I don't know what I can say to Julie, but I want to see both of them!"

For some unexplained but compelling reason, Bob knew what he had to do so he could accomplish that.

CHAPTER 5

David made arrangements to get off an hour early for a week so he could be home when Jonathan got out of school.

He had come home for lunch and was there when Miranda appeared. Melody decided to fall asleep in the guest bedroom. After conferring with David and Miranda, she closed her eyes and fell asleep instantly. Miranda moved her hands over Melody's body, and her spirit rose up. Miranda then took her hand, and they rose through the ceiling.

David thought, "That is so cool!"

He placed the spread over Melody's body. He bent over and lightly kissed her on the lips.

He said, "Enjoy yourself, Honey. You are just going to love your trip!"

He took a last quick look around before he closed the guest bedroom door. After locking the front door, he found himself whistling a little jingle as he got back into his car.

Driving back to work, David smiled.

He thought, "Melody is going to see and learn so much! I just wish both Jonathan and me could be with her! I would love to watch their eyes really pop open. I would give a pretty penny to be able to see her face when she first looks at Gorbandihar! Oh, well, if wishes were horses, beggars would ride."

David left work early as planned. When he arrived at home, he immediately began preparing supper.

"Let's see," he thought. "How about having hamburgers, macaroni and cheese, a salad, and some milk?"

Because he had missed his lunch, he now realized how hungry he was as he moved about the kitchen.

He thought, "What will I tell Jonathan when he asks where his Mom is or where she went? I don't want to lie to my son or make up an elaborate story. Besides, I hope he will be able to go to Gorbandihar soon anyway."

Using this reasoning, David finally decided, "I'll tell him the truth and explain everything to him as simply as I can."

At that moment, David heard the front door close.

"Mom, I'm home!" Jonathan said as he entered the house.

David looked into the living room.

He said, "Mom's not here, Son. Come into the kitchen."

Jonathan smiled upon seeing his Dad and said, "Hi! What are you doing home so early? Where's Mom?"

David responded, "Come on into the kitchen, and help me get our food onto the table. I'll tell you all about it."

They made small talk as they set the table and sat down. David said grace. When he had finished, Jonathan reached for the macaroni and cheese.

Jonathan began by questioning: "Why are you cooking, Dad? Is something wrong with Mom? She's not sick or something, is she?"

David held up his hand, palm towards him.

"Hold the questions a few minutes, Son," he said.

He served himself a hamburger and placed one on Jonathan's plate. After he had served both of them a salad, he took a drink of milk. ·

"We are both hungry, so let's eat first, OK? I promise, I'll answer any questions you have," he said.

Jonathan gave him a big smile as he dug in. With a mouthful of food, he just nodded his head in agreement.

When they were finished, David thought, "Now's the time to discuss this. I hope I can explain it so he can understand."

Aloud, he said, "Your Mom's not sick. I'm cooking because your Mom is taking a trip."

Jonathan looked at him wide-eyed and asked, "Where'd she go Dad? How long will she be gone?"

David smiled in response to his son's inquisitiveness and answered, "She'll be gone for three or four days. Do you remember that pretty lady, Miranda, who was here a couple of days ago?"

Jonathan said, "I remember her, Dad. She acted like she knew me, but I don't think I've ever met her before."

David laughed and said, "You don't remember having met her, but she has met you!"

Jonathan just stared back at him and said, "Dad, that does not make any sense at all."

David noted the confusion on Jonathan's face and said firmly, "I need to talk with you. I need you to listen very carefully. Before I start, I want you to promise me that you'll never talk about what I'm going to discuss with you...not to anybody, and especially Petey!"

Jonathan looked at his Dad because he had never spoken to him like that before.

"So this is a secret, and I cannot even tell my best friend, Petey?" he asked with a little grin.

David looked steadily at Jonathan and said, "No one at all, and I mean it! I want your promise."

"OK, Dad. I promise, cross my heart," Jonathan responded solemnly.

"OK, come with me," David said as he rose from the table and began moving towards the guest bedroom.

Upon entering the room, Jonathan saw his Mom on the bed. He ran over close to her. But before he could touch his Mom, David took his hand.

He spoke, "Son, Mom's body is here, but her spirit is on a Planet a long distance away from here with Miranda. The Planet is called Gorbandihar. I was there long ago and was given special powers. When you were born, these were transferred by my genes to you. Have you noticed that you can do things that others can't?"

Jonathan's eyes flew wide open and were shining with rapt attention.

"Yup. I had to use heat on a bully at school yesterday. He was pushing Petey around so I stopped him!" he said proudly.

"That's another matter which we will talk about later," replied David. "Let's go back into the kitchen, OK?"

During the next couple of hours, David told Jonathan all about going to Gorbandihar, He Who Summons, Miranda, the lessons he had learned, and of course about the Planet. Jonathan listened with fascination.

Finally, Jonathan asked, "So Miranda is a space alien?"

David laughed and said, "I asked her that very question when I was on Gorbandihar. You know what she told me?"

"What?" asked Jonathan.

"She said she wasn't—that I was on her Planet so I was the alien!" he exclaimed.

Jonathan laughed out loud.

"Well, what about Mom? Is she asleep? Will she be OK until her spirit returns to her body?" he questioned.

David responded, "Yes, she'll be just fine. We don't want to disturb her or let anyone else bother her. That's also why you must tell no one about this. By the way, when you were a baby, you were very sick with

Pneumonia. Miranda cured you. That's why she knows you, but you were too small to remember her. Once your Mom visits Gorbandihar and understands why they gave me the powers to heal and you received it from me through the genes, she will be all right with the idea of you and me going to Gorbandihar together."

Jonathan became so excited that he began jumping up and down in anticipation.

"You mean, you and me can go to this Planet Gorbandihar pretty soon?" he asked.

David took his hand and said, "Calm down, Son. We won't be going anywhere until Mom gets back. It will happen, though. You have my word on it, and you know I always keep my word, right? Just remember, this is our little secret. You can talk freely to Mom or me about this, but only when we're alone and when no one else can hear, OK?"

Jonathan nodded in understanding and said, "I'm glad you told me everything, Dad, because I was beginning to think I was really different from everyone else—you know, like I was a freak. I was worrying about it a lot!"

David responded, "You are different because you have the powers to heal. Later, you'll be very good at doing that as you learn to use your gifts when you receive your training. Otherwise, you're as normal as any other boy your age. That is why it is very important that you not use your powers any more—bullies or not—until you understand them better, OK? I am very serious about this."

"Yes, Dad, I'll do what you say," Jonathan promised.

"Remember, you can talk freely to Mom or me about this. Do you have any questions?" David asked.

"Not that I can think of right now," he replied.

Almost in the same breath, he asked, "Can I go play at Petey's house for a little while?"

David shrugged his shoulders and said, "You may go for two hours, but after that, I want you home for your bath. Do you have any homework tonight?"

"No, not tonight," he replied as he hurried to the front door and let himself out.

David looked after him and thought, "It must really be great to be young and have all that energy!"

He smiled to himself about that.

He went into the guest bedroom to make a quick check on Melody.

He knelt over, gave her a little kiss, and whispered softly in her ear, "I hope you're having a good time and learning a lot. I love you, Sweetheart."

With that, he eased out of the bedroom, closed the door gently, and headed for the bathroom to shower.

CHAPTER 6

Tapping the calendar with her forefinger, Julie realized, "I sent the Divorce papers first class mail six weeks ago. Since that time, I've not received a reply."

Her thoughts meandered: "This worries me because Bob might have moved, or he could be in another state. Who knows, he might even be dead!"

She picked up the phone and called her lawyer, Harvey Tuckerson.

He suggested, "You should wait a while longer because of mail service issues—forwarding due to change of address, and so forth."

She thought, "That is sound advice. I just need to give it more time."

Having made her decision, she said aloud, "I'll talk to David about the Divorce when I get off work."

Later that evening, she drove over to David's house and rang the door bell. Jonathan opened the door.

When he saw Julie, he smiled and exclaimed, "Hi, Grandma!"

She knelt down and opened her arms. Without hesitation, Jonathan ran into her arms for a hug. He loved her very much.

"How have you been, Sweetheart?" she asked as she hugged him.

"Fine," replied Jonathan.

"Is your Dad at home? And where is your Mom?" she asked.

"Oh, he's in the bathroom right now, and she's sleeping," he replied.

Julie stepped through the door and closed it behind her. The house smelled stale and musty.

She thought, "I know Melody is a great housekeeper. She always keeps this house freshly aired out, but it certainly isn't right now."

As she moved into the living room, she could see the bedroom doors were open. She saw Melody lying on the bed in the guest bedroom.

"She looks like she is, indeed, asleep. But why is she lying in the guest bedroom? That seems very strange!" she thought.

David came into the living room. When he saw his Mom looking questioningly into the guest bedroom, he felt instant panic.

"Oh, no, what can I say to her now?" he thought.

Julie noticed the look of panic on his face, which only made her even more uncomfortable.

He said, "Hi there!" as he came towards her with his arms open to give her a welcome hug.

As he embraced her, his mind groped desperately to control his fear. He realized he was not succeeding very well.

As their embrace ended, she pulled back, holding David's arms.

She looked into his eyes with a knowing look and said, "What's wrong with Melody, Son? Is she sick? I've never known her to nap during the daytime. And why is she sleeping in the guest bedroom? Maybe I'd better go get my stethoscope so I can check her out."

She turned and headed towards the door as she spoke.

David said quickly, "Wait, Mom! She's not sick. I'll explain everything. Jonathan, why don't you go over to Petey's to play for a few minutes?"

Jonathan replied, "OK, Dad, but I want to visit with Grandma, too."

David said, "It's all right. I'll call over there in a little while, and Elsa can send you back so you can do that."

"I'll see you soon, Grandma," promised Jonathan as he went out the door.

"Have fun," she said, blowing him a kiss.

David said, "Please sit at the kitchen table, Mom. I'll make us a cup of coffee. It's a long story, so I'll start at the beginning."

As he began making coffee, he started by telling her about his accident, his out-of-body experience, Gorbandihar, He Who Summons, and Miranda. He continued with an explanation of his powers, healing Melody, Miranda healing Jonathan, making gold, and healing Julie of her Cancer. As the story unfolded, Julie's face displayed shock, disbelief and wonder.

David continued, "Melody is out-of-body right now. Her spirit is on Gorbandihar with Miranda and He Who Summons. They want to show her many wonders and that Their intentions are simply to do good for mankind. Our people are just not ready to accept this advancement. That is why I must complete any healings in secret and usually at night. When Jonathan was born, neither Melody nor I knew that genetic transference had occurred. Now Jonathan has the powers, too! He's too young to realize its importance, but with guidance and training, he will be able to heal as well as I do."

Julie finally asked, "Do you realize how much money you could make with your abilities?"

He laughed and said, "Not one red cent, Mom. I'm strictly forbidden to charge anything for my healing—no favors or exchanges whatsoever!"

"I don't understand that at all. Can you truly do these things? Did you really heal me of my Cancer? How did you do it?" she queried.

"Do you remember all those hugs I gave you?" he asked.

"Yes," she responded, smiling. "You said you were making up for lost time."

He said, "That was just a cover so I could move my hands up and down your back to discover the problems and heal you. Do you remember feeling any heat from my hands when I hugged you?"

"No, not really," she replied. "I was just enjoying your hugs."

David took a coffee cup and dropped it intentionally to the floor. It broke into many pieces.

He laughed and said, "Just like Humpty Dumpty, remember?"

He gathered the pieces and began putting the cup back together. As he placed each piece, he fused it completely. Before he fused the last piece, he looked at his Mom.

"Put your hand by my right hand. Don't touch my hand, but put your hand close to mine. You will feel the heat," he stated.

Julie followed his directions and felt the heat radiating from the hand. Her eyes opened wide in wonder.

"That's quite amazing!" she exclaimed breathlessly.

David finished the process, picked up the cup, and handed it to her.

"I've never used my power for a demonstration before, but I want you to understand completely what I am saying to you. Now, see if you can find a crack anywhere in it," he instructed.

Julie made a very thorough inspection of the cup.

She said, "If I hadn't seen the cup break, or how you used your power to fix it, I would swear it had never been broken!"

Julie's eyes moistened.

"It's truly wonderful, David. You know what? I gave you life, and you've given me my life back. I love you and thank you so very much," she said.

David could not speak at that moment because he was all choked up.

He thought, "I'm so happy. To see Mom with the gratitude and love in her eyes is so much more precious to me than money. Helping others and improving their lives through healing is far more satisfying than that. Come to think of it, I am rich for I have a special feeling that no amount of money could buy!"

When he could speak, he looked into his Mom's eyes and said, "You must promise me that you will never tell anyone—and I do mean anyone—about this. It's important!"

She smiled and said, "Don't worry. I'll keep your secret."

"Thanks," he replied. "I'm not supposed to tell anyone, but I've had to tell Jonathan simply because I can't bring myself to tell lies to my son, especially when I want him to always tell the truth. I didn't want to lie to you, either. If I can't trust my immediate family, who can I trust?"

Julie squeezed his hand hard and said, "I'm glad you told me. It clears up a lot of little niggling questions I've had for years."

She continued, "By the way, I came over to talk to you about a decision I've made. Your Father and I have not been husband and wife for all these years, so I've decided to go forward with a Divorce. Six weeks ago, I filed for it and sent him the papers for his signature. I haven't heard anything from him yet. I don't know if he's received them or not. Perhaps he's moved, and the mail hasn't caught up with him. He may even be dead, for all I know. He was drinking pretty heavily. My lawyer suggested that I give it more time. That's what I've decided to do. But I wanted to talk with you to see how you might feel about it. You were only three years old when we left Texas, but I wanted to ask your opinion anyway."

David thought a few seconds and said, "I didn't know my Father, but from what you've told me, he's an alcoholic and very mean when he's intoxicated. After all, many years have gone by, so I really think you should do what you believe is right."

She said, "It will clear things up for us, especially where inheritance rights are concerned. I just didn't want you to be upset."

He replied, "In that case, you should finish it, just like you want. If it's all right with you, I'll call Elsa and have her send Jonathan home so he can visit with you for a little while."

David made the call. In a short period of time, Jonathan came running in through the front door with a big smile on his face, glad to see his Grandma again.

CHAPTER 7

Melody was completely awestruck during the trip to Gorbandihar.

She thought, "It's totally amazing!"

When they approached the planet, she gasped, "Oh my! If anything, David understated its beauty!"

Once landed, Miranda told Melody to follow her. They entered a room in a building complex.

"This is the very same room where I taught David his healing techniques," Miranda said.

Smiling at her, Miranda waved her hands over the console. Immediately, the panels came to life, displaying different scenes and locations on Planet Earth. All of the display screens were in beautiful color.

Melody gasped aloud as she gazed from screen to screen, with her eyes as big as silver dollars.

"David told me that your inhabitants were very far advanced over ours. Now I see what he means," she said softly.

Miranda waved her hands again. All of the screens but one went blank. The remaining screen displayed a symbol in color. She moved her hands over Melody's head, and a glowing golden crescent appeared to be floating in the air just above her hair.

Startled, she whispered, "Oh, my goodness!"

"Don't be alarmed," said Miranda in a calm voice. "It's simply a learning device to enhance the ability of your brain to absorb and understand more complex information. I am doing this to demonstrate how we trained David originally and how we wish to give Jonathan some very basic training. Are you willing to give it a try?"

Melody quietly nodded her head in assent.

"Good," replied Miranda. "It won't cause you any pain. David thought the process was, in his own words, the utmost in cool."

Melody could not help but laugh at Miranda's mimic of David's slang.

"If you're ready, we'll begin," said Miranda.

The screen flicked to a scene of the human body, showing the muscle structure on a frontal view, with a voice speaking in English, naming the different muscles as an arrow moved from muscle to muscle.

The voice stopped, however, when Miranda's voice began: "This device helps you to retain information. Right now, you're learning about basic anatomy. As your brain receives data, it will be enabled to absorb more at a faster rate. The tutor can then cover information more quickly. Right now, it is moving at its slowest setting," she said, laughing as she turned the screen off.

Rising from the control panel, she walked over to Melody and removed her crescent.

"See, I told you there would be no pain," she told her.

Melody smiled and said, "David is absolutely right!"

Miranda laughed and responded, "It's time for us to go for our visit with He Who Summons. I know He is anxious to meet you. Don't worry. You will like Him. He's very gentle and most wise."

"Does He know we are here?" asked Melody.

"Why, of course," replied Miranda.

"How?" asked Melody.

"He just knows. That's all," said Miranda with a smile.

Miranda set a brisk pace to the Receiving Room for He Who Summons.

Melody found herself observing the other beings on their way as she walked along.

They returned her friendly smile, but none of them tried to speak to her.

She just watched them in wonderment, thinking, "They seem to just float along instead of walk."

Her observations were cut short as Miranda said, "Here we are."

"Before we enter to meet Him, what do I do? Am I supposed to bow, kneel, or what?" asked Melody.

"Why, you're not supposed to do anything special. Just meet and visit with Him. You were invited here, and you are Our honored guest," explained Miranda.

They entered the dome covered archway at the entrance to an elegantly-decorated Receiving Room.

He Who Summons was at the other end of the huge room. When He looked up, He began moving towards them. He was wearing a multicolored, brocaded robe, with the sleeves dropping down to almost knee level. He held out His hand.

In response, when they were only a couple of feet apart, Melody reached out her hand to make contact with His outstretched hand.

He gently took her hand in His.

"I've been expecting you," He spoke in a normal, soft voice. "You must be David's wife, Melody, and also the mother of Jonathan," He stated.

"Why, yes, I am," replied Melody with a smile.

She thought, "I can't help it. His impish smile and twinkling eyes affect me this way."

He motioned towards comfortable-looking chairs. When the two of Them were seated, Miranda retrieved a chilled pitcher and commenced pouring their Native drink into tall glasses until they were almost full, handing one to each of Them before she, too, took a glass and sat down.

He Who Summons looked at Melody and said, "Welcome to Gorbandihar. How was your journey?"

"It was wonderful! I've never experienced anything so beautiful or exciting!" she exclaimed.

"That's good. I'm glad to hear it," He responded. "We want very much to make a good impression on you."

"I would just like to say thank you for inviting me. I'm happy to be here," she replied softly.

He continued, "I know Miranda has explained why We invited you to come. You can now see for yourself how We live on Gorbandihar. When David and you married and had Jonathan, I believed that the power We entrusted with David could be transferred genetically. I'm thrilled for Jonathan, but I can see that he needs some basic training, just to be sure he starts off on the right foot. Also, it's time to update David's training as well. Miranda will take you around and show you some of our more interesting locations. She's very knowledgeable in many areas so she can answer your questions. I hope you will enjoy your visit with Us."

A small bell began ringing, interrupting Their conversation. It continued to ring incessantly.

"I'm sorry," He said. "With regrets, I must cut Our meeting short as other matters of importance require My immediate attention. Miranda will show you your quarters for your stay. Enjoy yourself, and I hope to see you again soon."

He rose and smiled at them prior to moving through an open door.

Miranda stood up and said, "Come with me. I'll show you the quarters we prepared for you."

"Do you have daytime and nighttime, like we do on earth? Do you sleep at night like we do?" asked Melody.

"No to all of your questions," replied Miranda. "We have neither day, night, nor sleep periods."

Melody smiled and said, "We use sleep to rest and refresh our bodies."

"Yes, I know," replied Miranda, smiling kindly at her. "We have studied the lives and habits of Earthlings intensely for many of your Earth periods, or years as you call them."

"You mean that your bodies never get tired?" asked Melody in wonder. "You don't require food or rest at all? That is awesome!"

Miranda replied, "We refresh our bodies by periodically drinking our Native refreshment, which you just tasted. Did you like it? The flavor is much like one of your drinks, which you call mint-flavored tea. It keeps our bodies strong and fit."

"Yes, it was absolutely wonderful," replied Melody.

"Here we are," Miranda said as she opened a door.

She allowed Melody to enter first. The quarters were spacious. Even though the walls and ceiling were all a soft almond color, there were wall hangings of brightly-colored weaving and brocades to break up the plainness, just like the Receiving Room.

"It's very nice, and I appreciate your efforts very much," Melody said.

"Good! He Who Summons insisted that we prepare quarters for you, even though we will be so busy you'll probably not spend much time here. Come with me now. There's little time and so much to see," Miranda stated as she opened the door to go out.

CHAPTER 8

Bob Michaels looked at the map he had used on his trip to Colorado. As he sipped his coffee while waiting for delivery of his hamburger and fries, he gazed at it.

He thought, "Man, it didn't look like a long trip, but driving it has proven to be a lot further than I expected."

His hamburger and fries arrived. He gazed out of the window as he ate.

"It looks like it is a beautiful, sunshiny day. Maybe this trip will turn out to be a move for the better," he thought as he enjoyed his small meal.

The restaurant he had chosen was located in Aurora, Colorado, on East Colfax Avenue.

He thought, "After I finish eating, my first priority will be to find an inexpensive motel for a few nights. Next, I will need to find a job because what money I do have will not last long. Before I can begin to job hunt, I must have a place to leave my tools secure."

Bob finished his food, got up and left without tipping.

"I have to manage my money carefully," he thought as he walked out the door.

He looked at his watch and thought, "I'm going to drive along this street to check out the motels."

After he spent some time scouting, he chose one and pulled in to check the rates.

He thought, "It's already late evening, and I'm so tired from the trip. A shower and bed would really feel good!"

Bob talked with the Manager for a few minutes, settling on a rate for three days, with an agreement that he could have the same rate if he chose to stay longer.

He opened the door to his room and looked in.

"Well, it's nothing fancy, but it'll do for now," he said aloud.

He propped open the door so he could retrieve his suitcase, travel bag, and tools. The tools he stored in the clothes closet.

He thought, "My clothes can just stay in the suitcase for now."

He undressed and got into the shower.

"Oh, this hot water not only feels good, but it is very relaxing!" he said aloud.

He finally got out of the shower, toweled off, and laid down on the bed, still talking to himself: "Won't Julie be surprised when I go to see her? I wonder how David will react? Well, let's just keep first things first," he reminded himself. "In the morning, I'll get a paper and begin to look for a job. I'll even get an apartment before I try to see them. Tomorrow, I will begin my quest."

He closed his eyes, thinking of Julie's beautiful face in his mind's eye until sleep finally overcame him.

CHAPTER 9

David and Jonathan were watching television when the door bell rang.

"Keep your seat, Son. I'll get the door," said David.

When he opened the door, nobody was there, which perplexed him. When he turned around, he saw Miranda standing in the guest bedroom doorway. She smiled and put her finger over her lips to silence David, who smiled immediately from ear to ear. He knew that Miranda would enable Melody to re-enter her body. As soon as she performed that task, Melody rose and tip-toed into the living room.

"Jonathan!" she called.

When Jonathan heard his Mom's voice, he let out a squeal of delight and exclaimed "Mom—you're back!" as he jumped to the floor.

Upon seeing his Mom, he ran to her as fast as his legs could go. Melody opened her arms, bent over laughing, and grabbed him up in a huge bear hug, lifting him off the floor. She smothered his face with kisses.

She asked him, "Did you miss me?"

Jonathan looked at her with a big smile and said simply, "Yup!"

In truth, he did not know when he had been so happy.

Miranda and David laughed from the doorway at the reunion. Afterward they, too, moved into the living room.

David said, "Wait a minute, Sport. She has to save some of that sugar for me, you know!"

He put his arms around Melody, hugged her tightly, and then kissed her soundly.

"Welcome home, Sweetheart. We've missed you so much," he told her.

Melody had tears of joy in her eyes as she replied, "It's good to be back home!"

David turned off the television, and they all found a seat.

"Well, tell us all about it. I know Jonathan wants to hear everything, and it's almost his bedtime. I'm curious, too. Did you meet He Who Summons?" David asked.

Melody bubbled about her experiences on Gorbandihar and laughed as she recounted all the wonders she had encountered there. Jonathan was very excited, and his little eyes sparkled as he leaned towards his Mom. He was soaking up every word like a sponge. When Melody talked about traveling through space, and how beautiful and awe inspiring it was, Jonathan could stand it no more. He bounced off the sofa and stood before his Mom.

In a pleading little voice, he asked her, "When can I go there, Mom? I'd like to go right now!"

Miranda smiled at Jonathan's eagerness.

Melody spoke to him, "You simply can't go until you are out of school for the holidays."

She turned to Miranda and asked, "How long would he need to be there with David—in Earth time, please?"

Miranda responded, "I believe five of your Earth days would be enough for a first visit. When he's older, we can arrange for another visit. By then, he should be able to travel alone with me. Of course, the length of time involved would depend on how well he progresses."

Miranda smiled, looking at Jonathan.

"I'll learn good and quick," he boasted proudly.

He was beaming because of the attention being showered on him. His action brought laughter from both David and Melody.

Melody looked at the clock, turned to Jonathan, and said, "It's late and is well past your bedtime. Say good night to Miranda and Daddy. I'll tuck you in. You have school tomorrow."

"Aw, can't I stay up just a little while longer?" he asked.

"No, you know the rules," she replied.

He moved over to his Dad to give him a hug, and next he turned to Miranda.

"I'd go tonight if I could," he said.

Miranda smiled and said, "Good night, Jonathan. It will happen soon, I assure you."

He gave her a big smile and said, "OK. That's good enough for me!"

Melody took his hand and moved towards his bedroom.

"Please excuse me for a few minutes, won't you?" she said as they left the room.

"David," said Miranda, "whenever Jonathan has enough vacation time, all you need to do is say so out loud. Remember, our monitors? We'll receive your message immediately."

"Oh, I remember," he said, smiling. "But, as Melody told Jonathan, there won't be enough time until the Christmas Holidays."

Melody came back into the living room and sat down.

"Did I miss anything?" she asked.

"No," he replied, "I was just going to tell her that you and I need to discuss his holidays before we decide on the exact schedule."

Miranda rose, looked at both of them, and said, "When you've reached a decision, just let Us know. I'll take my leave for now."

Melody had risen to her feet as well and spoke to her, "Thank you for showing me your Home Planet of Gorbandihar and all the beautiful sights. I'll never forget them. Now, every time I look at the stars at night, I'll smile because I know that, on a Planet among them, you and He Who Summons are there."

Miranda smiled at her and replied, "You are most welcome. We enjoyed your visit, too."

After good byes were spoken, Miranda began rising towards the ceiling. They watched as she disappeared.

Melody looked at David, took his hand, and said softly, looking into his eyes, "I never dreamed something like this was possible. Why didn't you tell me sooner?"

"Frankly, my Dear, I was worried you might think I was off my rocker!" he said, laughing.

She laughed with him and said, "Now, I'll have to keep the secret too, or else everyone will think I've lost my marbles. Besides, no one would ever believe us anyway."

She reached up and gave him a big kiss and said with a smile, "Are you ready to go to bed yet?"

He reached around her with a big bear hug, picked her up, and said, "You betcha!"

CHAPTER 10

Bob Michaels succeeded in landing a job with a construction company. They were more than happy to hire a qualified carpenter and framer because jobs in the Denver Metro area were plentiful at this time. In fact, many companies could not find qualified workers to fill needed slots.

He went to work three days after his arrival in Aurora. To say he was happy would be an understatement.

"It feels good to be back to work," he thought, "and earning a paycheck doesn't hurt, either. Now I want to find a furnished apartment in close proximity to my job. I know that construction work often changes locations because that's simply the nature of it. Still, it won't hurt my wallet to start out close to my job. The next step for me will be to settle in for awhile. I'll need to prove my worth to my new boss and crew leaders—that I'm competent at my trade as well as reliable. This will take time, but to my way of thinking, this will work out best for me. There's no real hurry about my plans. After all, it's been a lot of years since I've seen Julie or my son. While I'm working, I can make some calls to locate Julie's work place. With any luck, I'll also locate David as well. He might still be with her, even though he's grown up now. Anyway,

I'll have the time to accomplish everything I want to do."

The days blended into weeks. Bob had rented a nice little apartment. He worked hard to accomplish step one—convince his boss and crew leaders that he was indeed an asset and worth keeping, and maybe later, even given a raise in wages.

Looking back over those few weeks, he thought, "It pleases me because everything seems to be falling into place for me now. I've made a lot of phone calls. I found that my wife works at Fitzsimons Army Medical Center right here in Aurora. Soon, I'll initiate another step in my plan—I'll call Julie!"

CHAPTER 11

David and Melody were having a long talk about the timing for going to Gorbandihar during the two-weeks' recess for the holidays, which had already begun.

He said, "He and I could go this first week and be back for Christmas, Honey."

"I don't know," she responded. "You know how important to me this family time is."

"Well," he said, chuckling, "I have an idea. I'd like to go during this first week of Jonathan's holiday vacation. Would you abide by our son's decision? He can be the tie breaker."

"OK, if he agrees with you, it could work out for me. With you two gone, I'll be able to decorate the tree and the inside of the house for Christmas. I'll have to wait until you get back to put up the outside lights, though," she declared.

David was grinning, and Melody threw a bath towel at him.

"Well, don't just stand there, grinning like a mouse eating cheese. Call him in here," she said.

To herself, she thought, "I'm pretty sure what Jonathan's answer will be. I'll be lonely with both of them gone for five whole days. Oh, well, they did get along without me for a few days, so I guess I'll be able to handle it."

David went out into the back yard to call Jonathan, who was playing with his large toy dump truck.

"Where's Petey, Son?" he asked, surprised to find him playing alone.

"Oh, he had to go to the dentist with his Mom. He said the dentist was going to put a filling in one of his teeth. How do they do that, Dad, and why?" asked Jonathan.

David laughed and answered, "Petey probably has a cavity. That's a spot on a tooth that is decayed. The dentist has to drill out the cavity to remove the decay and will have to put a metal filling into the hole. Come inside, now. Mom and I want to ask you an important question."

Jonathan followed his Dad into the house and went into the kitchen where Melody was busy cooking.

"What do you want to ask me?" Jonathan inquired as he reached for one of his favorite foods—a chocolate chip cookie.

"Leave that until after dinner," she said. "I don't want you to spoil your appetite."

"Aw, Mom," he retorted, "Can't I have a little one, please?"

She laughed, sat down, and said, "No, not even a little one until after dinner."

David took a chair and motioned for Jonathan to do the same.

With both of them seated, Melody began, "Your Dad and I have been having a discussion about this first week of your Christmas Holidays."

"It's about Gorbandihar, isn't it?" squealed Jonathan, jumping off his chair.

"Yes, it is," replied Melody in resignation, "but you need to sit back down and listen."

Jonathan sat down and looked from his Mom to his Dad, eagerly waiting.

She went on, "Your Dad wants the two of you to travel to Gorbandihar during this first week and be back for Christmas. I want you to stay here as a family for that week and go to Gorbandihar the second week. So, it's one to one. Since we are a family, you have the deciding vote. Which will it be, Son, go or stay?"

Jonathan was very bright, so he asked, "Do I still get presents when we get back?"

David and Melody burst into laughter.

Finally, when she could speak, she said, "Yes, of course, you'll get Christmas presents when you get home."

"Oh, good," he said, smiling. "In that case, I vote to go with Dad to Gorbandihar. I really want to see the things you and Dad saw, and I want to learn how to use my powers, too."

"That's settled then," said Melody as she smiled at them. "I want you to see Gorbandihar, Son. It's just that I'm going to miss both of you so very much. Go wash your face and hands for dinner because it's almost ready."

She began to set the table.

Jonathan jumped down from the chair and ran over to hug his Mom.

"Thanks," he muttered. "It's going to be all right. Besides, we won't be gone too long."

He released her and trotted towards the bathroom. He did not see the tears in Melody's eyes, but David did.

David moved over so he could slip his arm around her and kiss her on the cheek.

"I'm OK," she said as she wiped her eyes. "I'm just sad about it, that's all. When will both of you leave?"

"Probably in the morning. You know that you're going to have to come up with a reason why Petey can't see Jonathan. He's a pretty smart, persistent little boy," he spoke softly.

"We'll talk after dinner—after Jonathan goes to bed," she answered softly as well so little ears would not hear.

Dinner was a quiet affair. Small talk was held to a minimum so everyone could enjoy the food while it was hot.

Once everyone had their fill, Jonathan said, "I cleaned my plate, Mom—vegetables and all. Now can I have that cookie?"

She could not suppress a laugh as she handed the bowl of cookies over so he could get one. He checked them closely and chose the very largest one in the bowl. She poured him more milk to go with it.

David thought, "Anyone could see the love she has for him in her eyes."

Later, after Jonathan was asleep, Melody and David talked a long time. It was decided that she would call Elsa to tell her both David and Jonathan had come down with an illness and were bed ridden—that she did not know if it was catching or not, but she did not want to take any chances on Petey catching whatever it was.

David agreed that would be a good cover because neither Tom, Elsa nor Petey knew that David—and to a certain extent, Jonathan—could cure themselves.

David looked toward the ceiling and spoke out loud, "Miranda, Jonathan and I are ready to come to Gorbandihar early tomorrow morning."

He looked at Melody and said, "Miranda and He Who Summons can monitor me twenty-four hours a day, so they'll know it is time for us to come."

He put his arm around Melody's waist and moved towards the bedroom.

She leaned into him and said softly, "I probably don't need to say this, but I can't help it. Please take good care of yourself and our son."

"Don't worry, Sweetheart. We're going to be just fine. You have my word on it," he said, kissing her gently.

Melody was already up at seven o'clock. She was sitting at the kitchen table, contemplating her tea cup, deep in thought. She heard a sound so she lifted her head and saw Miranda standing there, smiling at her.

"Are David and Jonathan up yet, Melody?" she inquired.

"No, they are both still asleep," she replied.

Miranda looked at Melody, who already had tears in her eyes, and asked, "Are you going to be all right?"

"Yes, Miranda. Are you ready to take them?" she questioned.

"I believe so, because the sooner we start the training, the faster they'll be back with you," Miranda answered.

Miranda went into the bedroom and moved her hands over David. She called his name, and his spirit rose up from his body. She took his hand and went into Jonathan's room. She repeated the process with Jonathan. His spirit rose, and she also took his hand.

She told them, "Let's go, guys." She smiled at Melody and said, "We'll be back before you know it."

She looked upward, and they lifted off and disappeared through the ceiling.

"Too bad we can't do that with our real bodies," Melody thought as she adjusted the bed covers over Jonathan.

He had a little grin on his face. She bent over and kissed his cheek.

"He's probably dreaming about Gorbandihar," she thought, smiling. "He's wanted to go there for as long as he's known about it."

Next, she went into their bedroom and did the same thing, adjusting the covers over David, embracing him gently as she did so.

Afterward, she went into the kitchen to make another cup of tea so she could plan her conversation with Elsa.

CHAPTER 12

Bob worked hard at his trade. Everybody at his work site, including his boss, were not only happy with his work, but were very impressed with his ability.

As he worked along, he was thinking, "Today is the day I've been anticipating since I arrived in Aurora. Everything I've planned and all the steps I've executed have good results. When I get off work today, I'll go to my apartment, eat, and then call Julie on the new phone I've installed. Now that the time to make that call has finally rolled around, I'm experiencing hesitation because I still haven't figured out what I'm going to say to her. What will I do if she won't even speak to me? There's no denying that she wants this Divorce, and by now she's probably really angry because I haven't answered her. I wonder if she's found someone else? After all these years, I certainly do not have a claim on her because, during that time, I did not know where she was. I could not call her to try to re-establish a relationship or to even apologize for getting drunk and striking her hard enough for her to fall down to the floor! I could not send any money to help her with David's upbringing."

All afternoon, these thoughts played on his mind.

"I can't really blame my weakness with alcohol on anyone but myself. No one twists my arm to force me to drink. Left in the bottle, booze never hurt anyone. I know what getting drunk does to me. I understand from what others tell me later that I've got a really mean disposition then. All of this resulted in where I am right now—without Julie or David."

As time at work wound down towards quitting time, Bob worked steadily on, but he kept agonizing about what he was going to say to Julie.

He thought, "Maybe I should just call, apologize, and let her know I received the Divorce papers. I can tell her that I'm here in Aurora and that I sure would like to talk to her in person!"

Finally, he got off from work and drove to his apartment. After he had heated some chili and made a lunch meat sandwich to go with it, he opened a can of soda.

He said aloud, "It's not the best diet in the world, but at least it's hot and fills me up."

When he finished his food, he called Fitzsimons Army Medical Center and asked information to ring where she worked. The operator transferred him to the third floor, where an aid answered the phone.

"Could I please speak with Nurse Julie Michaels?" asked Bob.

"I'm sorry, but she is not on duty right now. May I take a message?" she responded sweetly.

"Could you please give me her home phone number?" he inquired. "It's very important."

"No, I'm sorry," replied the aid, "but we're not allowed to give out that information."

"OK," Bob responded, "thanks a lot anyway."

He hung up the phone and eyed the telephone directory.

He thought, "I wonder if she's listed in it?"

He thumbed through the white pages to the letter M section. Using his finger, he went down the page, looking for a "J."

"Sure enough, there's her name, address and phone number!" he said aloud.

He was becoming more anxious now than ever before.

He copied down this information and found the Metro street index and map. He located the street she lived on and looked for his own street address.

He thought, "Wow! The two addresses are probably no more than three miles apart! After all this time, we are very close."

He took a deep breath and dialed her number.

The phone rang three times. It seemed like an eternity, and then a female voice answered the other end and said, "Hello."

"Is this Julie Michaels' residence?" he asked.

"Yes, this is she. Can I ask who's calling?" she inquired.

"It's Bob, Julie. How are you?" he asked, hating himself instantly for asking such a dumb question.

"Bob? Bob who?" the female voice asked in a stern tone.

"It's Bob Michaels, Julie. I'm your husband," he said quietly.

There was a long silence on the other end.

He thought, "I wonder if the phone's dead?"

At last, she asked, "Bob, if it's you, why haven't you written or called concerning the Divorce papers?"

He responded, "I received the Divorce packet a few weeks back, but I've been very busy. Before I sign anything, I'd like to meet with you in person to talk about it."

She replied, "As far as I'm concerned, there's nothing to be said, and I'm not coming all the way back to Texas just for that. Besides, too many years have passed. Anything between us died on the vine a long time ago!"

"I'm not in Texas any more. I'm in Aurora now. I'm not going to try to talk you into anything. I've made a lot of mistakes in the past that I'm sorry for, but there's no reason we can't be civil to one another," he spoke softly. "If it's possible, I'd like to see David. After all, for better or worse, he is my son, too."

Again, there was a long silence.

"I'll have to think about this for a few days. How long will you be here in Aurora?" she asked.

He responded, "I've moved here. I have a good job, and I have my own apartment. I've already been here for four weeks. I've been working for the last three and a half weeks, so I'm not going anywhere."

Julie was shocked at this information, and she felt panic for a few moments while he spoke.

Now, she collected herself and said, "I'll still need time to think about all of this. You can call me back again, and I'll tell you what I've decided."

"OK, I'll do that. I hope my call hasn't upset you too much. If it makes you feel any better, it's bothered me, too, because I didn't know where to even begin after all this time. Good night," he said as he heard the click on the other end as she hung up without even saying good bye.

He held the phone in his hand for a long time, just looking at it until he finally placed it back in its cradle.

He thought, "Well, at least I called her. There are so many things I wish I'd said in a different way."

He had to run an errand to the service station for gas and a few other items.

As he climbed into the truck, he said, "Tomorrow's another workday, but I've finally made contact with her. I thought I would always be able to recognize her voice. Guess I was wrong about that, too! Time changes a lot of things."

CHAPTER 13

Jonathan's eyes were shining. He moved his head from side to side, trying to take in all the beauty of space as they traveled through it.

Once they approached Planet Gorbandihar, Jonathan was so excited that his Dad laughed hard and Miranda smiled.

When they landed, Jonathan pointed at a conveyance full of occupants who were being silently transported to some unknown destination.

"That's the kind of people carrier that Mom was talking about," he blurted to his Dad and Miranda.

She responded, "I believe it is, Jonathan. My, but you're very observant to spot that right away."

She motioned for them to follow as she moved at a steady pace down a maze of corridors. She stopped in front of a very ornate entrance.

"Are you ready to meet He Who Summons?" she asked.

"You mean we will actually be able to see Him?" asked Jonathan excitedly.

"Sure," replied Miranda. "Why not?"

David suddenly realized that he had not met He Who Summons either.

He thought, "Just like my son, I am also excited about this, and I'm looking forward to this meeting."

She turned to go into the dome-covered archway at the entrance to the Receiving Room, which was very large and open. Hanging brocaded tapestries and symbols softened the beige-colored masonry.

"Wow!" exclaimed Jonathan. "This is awesome. This would be a great place for roller skating."

Miranda laughed and asked, "Do you roller skate?"

"No," he said. "I don't have roller skates yet, but I could learn how in no time at all. I know I could."

One of the doors opened at the other end of the room as He Who Summons entered. He had long white hair and wore colorful, flowing robes. He moved towards them, smiling.

When He was a couple of feet from them, He stopped and spoke in a soft voice, "Welcome back to Gorbandihar, David. This young man must be Jonathan."

He gave Jonathan a big smile and asked him, "Did you enjoy your trip here?"

Jonathan looked into He Who Summons' eyes and said, "The trip was awesome! It's a hundred times better than standing on Earth and looking into the star-filled heavens on a clear night! When we were coming in, I saw your Planet. As we got closer, I could actually see the spires and buildings! It's very beautiful, just like my Mom said it was."

He listened to Jonathan and laughed at his enthusiasm.

"We agree. Thank you for the compliment," He responded.

Turning to David, He said, "Well, you have a very wonderful son. I'm glad you and I finally have an opportunity to meet and get to know each other."

He extended His hand and smiled, "I believe this is your way of saying Hello."

David took His hand and firmly shook it as he smiled and said, "Yes, it is, and thanks for inviting us. Jonathan has been looking forward to this with great anticipation. He's very fond of Miranda already and is looking forward to his training." He laughed and said, "For him to look forward to any schooling is a first for him."

He Who Summons looked at them and said, "I believe Miranda might have a few surprises in store for both of you."

He nodded at Miranda as He spoke.

Her face lit up into a radiant smile as she responded, "I just may at that, Master."

"Well, We are happy to have both of you here. I believe she has arranged some advanced procedures and techniques for you, David. She's prepared basic instruction for Jonathan as well," He said as He glanced at His folder. "Do you have any questions?"

Jonathan raised his hand as a reflex action.

When He Who Summons nodded at him, he blurted out, "Don't you guys have any little children like me?"

David was at a loss for words and was going to attempt to intercede on behalf of his son's brashness when He Who Summons started laughing, along with Miranda.

He answered, still laughing, "Why, yes, we do have young ones—as you shall soon see."

He rose, as did Miranda.

"There's a lot of information waiting for both of you to absorb. I'm sure she is anxious to get both of you started," He said as

He smiled. "I'll see all of you later," as He nodded at Miranda.

She acknowledged He Who Summons with a slight bow and turned, motioning for David and Jonathan to follow her. Once they were outside the Receiving Room, she led them towards the Advanced Learning Center.

"How about it, guys?" she asked, slipping into vernacular that was easy for them. "Are you ready to begin?"

"I am," said Jonathan quickly.

"I am, too. There's no reason to delay. Besides, that is what we came for," replied David.

"All right. Please follow me, and we'll get started," she said as she led the way into a large room equipped with many screens on the walls.

She motioned for David to occupy a comfortable chair in front of a large screen and console. She moved her hands over the console, and it came to life with lights blinking. The screen also lit up, displaying colorful pictures.

"Look at that!" Jonathan exclaimed.

"Oh, I almost forgot," she said as she moved her hands above David's head.

Immediately, a glowing golden crescent appeared over his head.

Jonathan jumped up and down in excitement.

"Do I get one, too?" he blurted.

Miranda laughed as she said, "You'll be getting one soon enough."

She instructed David on how to advance and reverse the screen so he could set his own pace of absorption.

"You'll probably do much better if you start slow at first. Here's the dial you turn to advance the speed. Do you have any questions before I take Jonathan to his own Learning Center where I can get him started?"

"None that I can think of at the moment," he replied, already absorbed in the screen before him.

"All right," she responded.

Half turning to Jonathan, she said, "Let's go. I have something special to show you before we start your instruction."

They walked for a short while and finally went into a clear tube unlike anything Jonathan had ever seen. They were lifted up until Miranda waved her hand over a panel of blinking lights. The lifting stopped. Together, they stepped out of it.

Miranda opened a big door, and Jonathan followed her into a large room.

Jonathan thought, "Oh, here are some younger beings—some my size, some larger, and one is smaller. I'm counting eight in all. Three of them are tossing sparkling balls back and forth between themselves. That looks like fun!"

"Is this a class you're teaching?" he asked with a big smile.

"No," she replied. "These are my children. They are playing much like you do on your Planet Earth."

"You have eight already? You sure don't look old enough to have that many!" he exclaimed in genuine surprise.

Miranda laughed.

"I'll have you know, my young Earthling friend, that as you tell time on your Planet, I'm one hundred and sixty-one years old. I should have many more children, as most females on our Planet do."

Jonathan's mouth opened wide in amazement.

Miranda waved her hands over Jonathan's head, and a glowing golden crescent appeared over his head.

"I'm giving you this so you will remember their names," she said as she motioned for them to come forward.

When they had formed a line before her, she spoke, "The oldest is Eroc, who is thirty of your years in age. The next is Roan, twenty years; Latox, who is eighteen; Jakin, fifteen years; then we have Elo—she's thirteen years; Notan, who is twelve years; Rendy, who is ten years; and last we have Breta, who is eight years."

Jonathan took a step forward and said, "My name is Jonathan, and I'm eight years old as we measure time on my Planet Earth."

Eroc looked at Jonathan and said, "We have studied Earth, among other Planets. We know many Earthlings like games played with differently-shaped balls. Do you like such games too?"

"Yes," replied Jonathan, "I do—a lot!"

"Maybe we can play sparkle ball?" asked Eroc, as he looked hopefully at his Mother.

Miranda shook her head in answer as she said, "Jonathan may be able to play sparkle ball later, but right now, we must begin his training. He can only be here for a short while."

"OK," responded Eroc. "We'll play later," he promised Jonathan.

With that, Miranda took Jonathan's hand, and they moved towards the entrance door.

When she opened the door, she spoke to Eroc, "I'll be back later. I have duties to attend to for He Who Summons."

Eroc touched his right hand to his forehead, which was a simple gesture of acknowledgment.

"Gorbandihar children are completely different from Earth children," thought Jonathan as he went through the door. "I've got so much to learn!"

As they walked, Jonathan paid Miranda a compliment: "Your children are very nice, and they are sure lucky to have a Mom like you."

"Why, thank you," she said, smiling at him. "OK, we'll turn here. It's just a short walk now to where we need to go."

They arrived in a brightly-lit room inside a large complex. Miranda waved her hands over the console. Screens came to life with colorful pictures of Earth. Jonathan just stood there, looking from screen to screen in total wonder.

He said excitedly, "This is so cool!"

She just smiled at him and said, "This is where your Dad trained years ago, and he used that very same phrase. Please sit down here."

She waved her hands again. An elementary program started on the monitor in front of him.

She stated firmly, "Please pay close attention now, Jonathan. The golden crescent will help you understand the information so you can remember it."

"This stuff sure looks complicated," he said.

"You'll understand it easily," she replied. "I'll be right over here in this chair with another monitor. I also have some work to do."

Jonathan settled into the comfortable chair, utterly fascinated with the pictures and information on the screens.

Smiling to himself, he thought, "This has got to be the coolest thing ever!"

CHAPTER 14

Julie had gone over to David's house with every intention of speaking to her son about Bob coming to Aurora and that he wanted to see him.

When she rang the door bell, Melody answered the door. She appeared to be agitated.

"What's wrong?" asked Julie, stepping inside and giving her a big hug.

Melody felt anxious about telling her a lie. She felt like she was walking on an emotional tight rope.

She thought, "I'll try the little ruse David and I discussed earlier. Maybe she'll believe it. I certainly don't have time to think up something else."

Out loud, she said quickly, "David and Jonathan are coming down with something. I don't know what yet. They are in bed, resting."

Julie said, "Oh, my, we'll just see about that."

She immediately turned and went out to her car to retrieve her stethoscope before Melody could stop her.

When she came back into the house, she said, "Let me quickly check them out. If they need a doctor, we'll get them to the hospital."

"But," stammered Melody, amazed at this quick turn of events, "you might be exposing yourself to whatever it is."

"Don't worry about that. I'm exposed every day at the hospital," she responded.

With that, she went into Jonathan's room first. She checked his lungs and blood pressure.

"Well, they're normal," she thought.

She felt his forehead and neck.

She stated quietly, "He is normal to the touch, with no fever, and he's breathing normally. He appears to be sleeping."

Next, she went into David's room and repeated the process.

"He's also perfectly normal. They are both just sleeping peacefully," she said softly.

She returned to the living room where Melody was nervously waiting.

"What's going on? There's nothing wrong with either of them," she stated quietly.

Melody knew it was useless to try to fool her mother-in-law.

"Would you please come into the kitchen so I can tell you all about it," she said.

The two went into the kitchen. Melody busied herself making cups of hot tea.

She was thinking about where to begin and feeling in a quandary about how to proceed.

Julie saw how uncomfortable Melody was and asked, "They're having an out-of-body experience, aren't they?"

It was a statement, more than a question.

Melody's jaw dropped in shock.

"How did you know?" she asked.

Julie laughed and responded, "David told me when your body was on the bed and your spirit was on Gorbandihar. He made me promise to not tell anyone, ever. But it's all right to talk to you because you already know."

Melody smiled and said, "It looks like the joke is on me. I am so relieved that you know. I just wish he had told me about informing you, and I wouldn't have had guilt feelings about lying to you! That stinker! Just wait until he gets back!"

"Oh, don't be too hard on him. He just probably forgot," Julie responded.

Melody served the tea and sat down.

"I'm so sorry for the deception. Will you please forgive me?" she asked.

Julie reached across the table and patted her hand gently as she answered, "It's all right. No harm's been done."

"Well, they will be home in four more days. I'll be so glad," Melody said, smiling brightly. "We're going to have a wonderful Christmas. Will you please help me decorate the tree and the inside of the house while we wait for their return?"

"Of course, I will. That will be great, and we'll have so much fun," she said as she looked at Melody and smiled as well.

She thought, "It is so nice, just sitting here, talking with my daughter-in-law at the kitchen table. I need to talk with someone about my own problem and dilemma. I believe I can go ahead and confide in her."

Aloud, she said, "I wanted to speak to David about a couple of important things. I've already told him that I had filed a petition for Divorce from his father. We haven't been husband and wife since David was three years old. David is all right with my decision. Anyway, about two months ago, I had a lawyer prepare the petition. I mailed it to Bob for his signature. To my knowledge, he still lived in Corpus Christi, Texas."

Melody got up and put the tea kettle back on a burner and got out two more tea bags.

"Please go ahead," she said as she regained her chair.

Julie continued: "Well, the other night, I received a phone call. I just automatically thought it was someone from the hospital. You cannot imagine my surprise when I found out it was Bob Michaels on the other end of the phone! He wanted to talk about our Divorce. I told him that there was no way I was going to go all the way back to Texas! He told me that I wouldn't have to do that because he was in Aurora! He told me he had found a job, had an apartment, and wanted to meet with me. He also said he wanted to see his son. I told him I needed a few days to think about that. Of course, I wanted to talk with David as well about seeing him and see what he thinks. I'll just have to stall Bob for another few days."

Melody listened quietly, and now it was her turn to pat her mother-in-law's hand. She got up, poured more hot water into their cups, and added the tea bags.

"This must be very traumatic for you," she said. "Is there anything I might do to help you?"

Julie took a sip of her tea and replied, "No, there's nothing you can do, but you've helped me already by just being here and listening to me. It's very nice to have someone with whom to discuss my problem. It just keeps going around in my mind, making me crazy."

Melody commented, "Well, you don't need to do that any more. You can come over anytime at all. You know our door is always open to you. I'll just be glad when David and Jonathan get back though. It's just too quiet in this house with them gone."

Julie laughed and said, "But half of them are still here."

Melody laughed too and stated, "Yes, but not the good half!"

Julie rose, looked at her, and spoke, "Thanks for letting me bend your ear. I had better be getting home now. I have a few little things to do before going to bed. I have to work tomorrow, as usual. There's no rest for the wicked, you know," as she winked at her.

Melody walked her to the door.

As Julie walked onto the porch steps towards her car, Melody said softly, "Good night, Mom. You know we love you."

Julie turned, smiled brightly, and said, "Now I like the sound of that. Good night. I'll see you again after work tomorrow. After all, we have to get the tree and the inside of this house decorated before they return, don't we?"

She then continued towards her car as Melody waved at her from the porch.

Melody thought as she turned and went inside, "Now that is an interesting turn of events. I wonder where David put those Christmas decoration boxes?"

CHAPTER 15

Miranda spent more time with Jonathan, teaching him the power at his level of comprehension. While she instructed him, she also showed him many of the interesting sites on Gorbandihar.

During his instruction, she placed a receiver-transmitter on his neck just behind his ear.

She thought, "Jonathan, or anyone else for that matter, won't even notice because of its small size and location. It will look just like a wart. But now we'll be able to monitor him also. We just have to do it differently from David because he was born with the power. This will be very important as he grows, so David readily agreed to this."

She even found time for Jonathan to play with her children, as promised.

She thought, "It's enjoyable to watch them play and exchange ideas. He is very likeable, and my children enjoy his company very much."

Miranda smiled as she watched them interacting.

She thought, "He can ask so many questions. He wants to know about everything he thinks about or sees that he doesn't understand. Some of his questions are laughable, but others are actually profound, coming from one so very young. Both David and Jonathan have now covered substantial information. I am certainly most pleased with how their programs have turned out."

The day for the completion of instruction had arrived. It was time for them to go see He Who Summons again.

As they entered the Receiving Room, He was waiting for them.

He said, "I do hope you have enjoyed your visit here on Gorbandihar. I am so very pleased with the progress both of you have made!"

He opened two identical boxes, and withdrew two beautiful medallions about as large as a half dollar. They shone like gold and were on very intricate gold chains. He placed one around David's neck. Next He turned and winked at Jonathan as He placed a medallion around his neck.

He stated, "These are a token of Our friendship for you both. I hope you like them and will keep them always. I know it is time for you to return to Earth, but you will be back, you know."

As they left the Receiving Room, He Who Summons waved at them in the Earthling gesture signifying good bye.

Miranda waved her hand at Him and laughed as she thought, "I can use Earthling gestures, too."

She took hold of one of each of their hands, and they began to rise. As they rose higher and higher, Gorbandihar looked smaller and smaller. Quickly, it became just a dot in the distance. It seemed like the journey home happened in just a twinkling of an eye.

They arrived back on Earth and were standing in the living room.

David turned to Miranda and said, "What's next?"

She just smiled in response and replied, "You already know."

David thought about that for a moment and responded with a smile, "Yes, I guess I do at that. Thanks so very much!"

Miranda was already rising up towards the ceiling, gave them a wave, and promptly disappeared.

David placed his finger over his lips while looking at Jonathan. They had arrived home at night.

David thought, "Melody will be asleep. There's nothing to be done that can't wait until morning."

He whispered into Jonathan's ear, and they went into his room. He waved his hands over his son's physical head, and Jonathan's spirit re-entered his body. He was now fast asleep.

David went into his bedroom. He could see that Melody was sound asleep, so he repeated the process and was asleep instantly as well.

When morning came, Melody arose from bed and stretched.

She looked at David's body, thinking, "I wish that they were home. I miss them so very much!"

As she turned to go out of the bedroom, she heard David's voice say softly, "Good morning, Sweetheart!"

She thought it might be her imagination until she turned to look at him. He was sitting up in the bed, smiling at her. With a shriek of happiness, she dove across the bed. She kissed him passionately, and he put his arms around her, hugging her tightly.

Neither of them noticed a small figure standing in the doorway with tousled hair.

"I'm glad to be home again! What's for breakfast, Mom?" he said with a big smile.

Melody laughed with joy.

"You are back!" she exclaimed.

She jumped off the bed, took a couple of steps and grabbed Jonathan into her arms. She laughed as she smothered his face with kisses.

"Aw, Mom," he sputtered. "We weren't gone that long."

David was laughing, too.

She asked, "What is that around your necks? They are beautiful!"

They looked down, and then they looked at each other, with a big smile on their lips.

David responded, "Why, He Who Summons gave us these as a token of Our friendship. What do you know, even though only our spirits were there, the medallions actually made it back to Earth from Gorbandihar!"

Jonathan picked his up, looked at it, and said, "Cool!"

David thought, "That apple certainly did not fall far from the tree!" as he smiled contentedly at the scene before him as Melody tickled Jonathan.

CHAPTER 16

Doctor Dan Hollis arrived home, and Betty came out of their son's bedroom to greet him home with a kiss as she always had done since they were married.

"Hi, Darling," she said, laying a square plastic container on the table.

Dan could see it had ice cubes and a wash rag inside as she reached up to kiss him.

After their embrace, he asked, "What's with the ice and wash rag, Honey?"

She responded, "Brandon is running a temperature again, and he seems listless. You know, he doesn't seem to have any energy either."

Dan saw the worried look on his wife's face.

"That has happened pretty often these last two or three weeks, hasn't it?" he asked.

"Yes, and I'm worried about him," she said softly.

Dan could tell she was close to tears so he went into his son's room. He placed his hand on Brandon's forehead as he checked his pulse. His forehead was hot to the touch. His face was flushed, and his breathing seemed to be forced.

He returned to the kitchen where Betty was and said, "I think maybe we should go ahead and take Brandon to the hospital now so we can find out what, if anything, is wrong with him. We can begin taking x-rays and tests. We won't be able to get any results on the blood work until tomorrow, but we can read the x-rays tonight."

Immediately, he saw the worried concern on her face so he spoke gently, "I know you'll agree that the sooner we begin, the sooner we'll know."

She nodded her head in agreement as she said, "You haven't had anything to eat yet, so I'll make you a sandwich to bring with us, OK? "

He could see a little relief on her face. He put his arm around her and pulled her close to him.

He said as he kissed her cheek, "Don't you worry about this now. Let's get him to the hospital and gather information, OK?"

He went into Brandon's bedroom. He cradled his son, wrapped him in a blanket, and carried him to the car. Betty got into the rear seat and helped Dan make him comfortable. His little head was resting on her lap, and he had not even awakened.

Dan started the car and began driving towards the hospital.

He thought, "I don't want to alarm her, but for once I am relying on my intuition. If it is proven false, no harm's been done. I would rather err on the safe side."

When they arrived at the Emergency Room, Dan picked up Brandon and brought him in, with Betty on his other side, holding his little hand. He noticed that Doctor Sam Rogers was on duty.

Dan smiled at him and thought, "I'm glad it is Sam. We not only know each other, but we've worked side by side in the past. I know he is an efficient and competent professional."

Sam returned his smile and said, "Hello. What brings you here tonight?"

"Our son, Brandon, does not feel well. I'd like you to check him out," he responded.

He laid him on a surgical bed in a curtain-enclosed area so they could begin the necessary tests. Very quickly, they obtained his pulse, which was elevated. His temperature was now one hundred and two degrees. They began charting the information. Doctor Rogers called for an x-ray technician as Dan filled out the necessary forms.

The technician came to confer with Doctor Rogers as to which x-rays were to be taken. Afterward, he pushed Brandon's gurney towards the elevator. Betty walked alongside with her hand on her son's arm.

Dan said to Sam, "He's been running a fever off and on for several weeks. Betty is telling me that he now seems listless and does not have any energy."

Sam stated, "The x-rays of his chest will eliminate or verify a couple of diagnoses that present these symptoms. But you know that already, don't you? At that time, if we have to do so, we can proceed from there."

"You're right. It's just that the waiting is so hard. I know now how parents feel when they are waiting for news about their loved ones," Dan said softly, with a catch in his throat.

Sam smiled at him and said, "I think I understand what you are saying, but I am still a single man. It must be hard, though."

Forty-five minutes had elapsed when the technician returned with Brandon. Betty was carrying the oversized Manila envelope containing the x-rays.

His eyes were open now and looking at everything in a very puzzled manner.

Dan walked over, touched his son's shoulder, and said, "It's going to be all right. Don't be afraid, OK? We are right here."

Sam and Dan looked for a long time at the chest x-rays.

Finally, Sam spoke, "Well, his lungs are clear with no evidence of Pneumonia, so something else must be causing his fever. We can do a blood draw, but we won't get the results until late tomorrow morning or possibly early afternoon. Do you have any other suggestions?"

"No," Dan responded. "You've been very professional. If it's all right with you, after the blood draw, we'll take Brandon home."

"That will be just fine," Sam said.

He called a nurse over to give her instructions. Very shortly, she moved over to Brandon and prepared to draw blood.

Betty watched her every move closely, thinking, "Actually, she's very professional. I don't know her and have not seen her before, but there are a lot of new personnel at the hospital. I can see she is doing a good job."

Dan thanked Sam and picked up his son. He motioned for Betty, who moved quickly to the door so she could hold it open for them.

As they were driving home, Betty thought, "I want to ask about the x-rays, but I think I'd best keep quiet for now. After Brandon is put back into his own bed, we will be able to talk freely. It must not be too serious, or they wouldn't have allowed Brandon to come home. I pray it's not because he is so very precious to me! I've waited for a long time to have a child of my own!"

Once home, they put Brandon back to bed. Afterward, they both went into the kitchen, hand in hand.

"Do you want some hot tea?" she asked.

"No thanks," he replied. "I'll just have a glass of milk."

She gave him a glass of milk and turned on a burner under the tea kettle. She sat down across from him.

"What did you find out?" she asked.

He looked into her blue eyes, thought for a moment, and replied, "His chest is clear, so we can write off Pneumonia. Maybe his blood work results will reveal something tomorrow. We'll just have to wait and see."

She was a very good nurse so her thoughts continued: "I realize some of the possibilities because of the symptoms. There's no need to mention them to him because he knows them far better than I do. I have a sneaking suspicion that's the reason he wanted to take him to the hospital tonight rather than wait till tomorrow."

Dan reached across the table, took her hands in his, and said, "We are going to tackle whatever it is together, Honey. Regardless of whatever it might be, we'll do it hand in hand, along with our son, come what may. But for right now, I'm going to get ready for bed. It's been a long day."

He rose to go into their bedroom.

She stood up and said, "I'll be along in a minute."

She went into Brandon's room to check on him one more time before going to bed herself.

She leaned over him, smoothed his hair, kissed his forehead gently and said, "Good night, my sweet son. God is going to help us find out what is wrong with you, and He will help us with whatever it is. We love you so very much."

With tears in her eyes, she turned and went towards their bedroom, praying, "God, I just know you are listening. Please help us find the answer!"

CHAPTER 17

Bob dialed Julie's number and waited patiently until she answered the phone.

"Hello," she said.

"Hello, it's Bob again. If I'm not mistaken, it's been five days now since we've spoken. When can we meet to discuss the Divorce? When can I see David?"

She responded, "Well, I have come to a decision. After discussing it with my lawyer, we decided that there is no reason to do that. The paperwork is very clearly written. All you need to do is sign where the red 'X' appears on the papers. He will take the remaining steps to complete the process and send you a finalized copy. Of course, I'll also get one. That will be it. It will be over between us. It should have happened a long time ago."

There was a long silence on the line.

He thought, "This wasn't the result I'd hoped for. It sounds so final. I guess I'll have to try another angle."

"Have you found someone else?" he asked timidly.

"That's none of your business. Is there anything else?" she asked in a business-like manner.

"Yes, there is. When do I get to see my son?" he asked.

She answered, "Whenever he agrees to it, I guess. I don't even know if he wants to see you at all. It's been many years, and you have not been a part of his life. You can find him in the phone book if you want to contact him."

Bob heard a loud click on the other end.

He thought, "There's a real finality to it when someone hangs up on you like that!"

He grabbed the phone directory and looked under Michaels. He realized that, when he had looked for Julie's number, he had completely skipped over any other listings.

Aloud, he said, "There's a listing for David and Melody Michaels! Well, what do you know, my son has gotten married!"

Grabbing a note pad, he wrote down their address and phone number.

Looking at the information, he formed his next plan.

He thought, "I am finally going to see them. I'll do that tomorrow when I get off work. I wonder what he looks like now? Will his wife be pretty?"

He laughed as he prepared for bed, thinking, "Tomorrow, I'll find the answers to both these questions."

Bob went to work the following morning, carrying clean clothes in anticipation, thinking: "I plan to change after work so I can be neat. After all, today's the day I'll finally see my son and his wife."

When work was over for the day, Bob had changed his clothes and was getting ready to leave when a couple of his co-workers came over. They started kidding him about his clothes.

"You got a hot date tonight?" asked Harry.

"No," Bob replied simply.

"We're going to our favorite sports bar for a burger and fries. Want to come with us?" Harry asked.

"Nah, I'd better not. I'm going to see someone," he said.

"Heck, you need to eat something anyway," replied Harry. "They make a great hamburger there."

Bob thought about it a moment or so, thinking, "I am hungry."

Aloud, he asked, "How far is this place?"

"Aw, it's only a couple of miles from here," Harry replied. "You can follow us there in your truck."

"OK—I will," Bob said.

In no time, they were parked outside the Point After Sports Bar. As they stepped inside, Bob could see all the sports posters and memorabilia on the walls. The bar was already fairly busy. It obviously was a favorite watering hole for workers after-hours. There were different foods on the various tables.

"Man, this reminds me just how hungry I am at this moment!" he thought.

There were three waitresses on the floor. All of them were pretty, wearing skimpy outfits and showing a lot of leg.

Harry ordered beer and burgers for himself and his close friend, Rock.

"How about it, Bob? Do you want a beer?" he asked.

He answered, "Sure, why not?"

The waitress asked if he was ready to order. He chose a fried chicken basket with fries to go with the beer.

In no time at all, what was to have been one or two beers became a table full of empties. Bob and Harry were exchanging jokes, while Rock just laughed.

Harry said, "You know what we need now, don't ya? Let's get some boiler makers— you know, shots of Vodka and just drop 'em into the beer."

Before Bob knew it, he had drunk a lot more than he had intended to without realizing it.

He looked at his watch and rose unsteadily to his feet and said in a slurred voice, "Guys, it's six forty-five. I've got to go. It's getting late."

After throwing a five dollar bill on the table for a tip, he winked at the waitress as he left the bar.

While checking the address, he got into his truck and then started driving.

He thought, "My speech is a bit slurred, and I feel a little tipsy. Otherwise, I'm just fine. Besides, I ate a good meal before I drank, didn't I?"

Once he located the address, he parked the truck at the curb—quite lop sided, but he, of course, did not notice. He stood waveringly for a few moments beside his truck.

He thought, "Julie did not have any reason to just hang up on me. That makes me mad!"

Unaware that the alcohol was already beginning to work on him, he staggered up to the front door. He knocked loudly on the door and waited.

The door was opened by a very pretty young lady.

She said politely, "Can I help you?" as she gazed at him.

"Are you Melody Michaels?" he asked, trying to control the slur in his voice.

"Yes, I am," she replied, easily catching the slur.

"Well, I'm Bob Michaels, David's Father," he said simply. "Is he at home now?"

She looked at him warily as she replied, "Yes, he's in the living room with our son, Jonathan."

"David's son," he repeated until he made the connection through the stupor in his mind. "Why that means I'm a Grandfather! May I see them?" he asked.

"Yes," she said, reluctantly holding the door open for him to enter.

As he passed her, she could smell the stench of both beer and alcohol on him. It alarmed her.

David and Jonathan were watching "I Love Lucy" on the television.

"Look who's here," she said as they entered the room.

David rose from the sofa and looked at the man standing there for what seemed like an eternity.

Finally, he spoke, "Do I know you?"

Bob looked at him, thinking, "I just cannot believe how big he is!"

Aloud, he said with a slur, "I'm your Father. Why, the last time I saw you, you were a little boy! You were no bigger than this," as he held his hand a couple of feet above the floor.

Melody was still in the opening between the entry way and the living room.

She thought, "This interchange between a father who never really knew his son and vice versa is so very strange!"

David responded, "I don't remember you at all. I guess my question is, why did you even want to meet me after all these years? I mean, why even bother? You never wanted to see me before!"

Ignoring David's negative response, Bob looked at Jonathan and asked, "Is this my Grandson?"

David replied, "Yes, he is, but he's never met you."

Bob looked at Jonathan and ordered gruffly, "Come over here."

The boy hung back, making no effort to get off the sofa. He could sense that something was terribly wrong, but he did not know what it was.

"Don't be afraid. Let me have a look at you," Bob insisted, the meanness showing in his voice.

Jonathan did not move.

"I'm your Grandfather. You do as I say!" he gritted from between his teeth.

David commanded, "Stop it! You are a stranger to him! What do you expect?"

Bob looked at David and said with a slur, "Actually, I didn't expect anything because I didn't even know you had gotten married and had a son. Look, I need your help. Your Mom wants a Divorce from me after all these years. She even filed papers. Now she doesn't want to talk to me about it! I need you to talk to her for me—convince her that she should talk to me first!"

David looked Bob straight in the eyes and spoke firmly, "Mom is perfectly capable of making her own decisions. It's basically between the two of you. It's none of my business!"

Bob was getting angrier by the minute and shouted, "You mean you won't help me at all?"

David responded furiously, "No! Why should I? You've had nothing to do with my life up to now. Suddenly, you show up at my house intoxicated, scare my son, and say you want my help. I'd say you certainly have a lot of audacity!"

Before he realized what he was doing, Bob crossed the living room floor in an angry, drunken daze, grabbed David by the throat, and began squeezing hard.

"I'm your Father," he roared, "and you'll show me some respect!"

He increased his grip on David's throat, squeezing harder.

David was caught off guard, but before he could react, Jonathan leaped from the sofa, ran up to Bob, and grabbed his right leg.

"You can't hurt my Dad, you big bully!" he shouted as his hands brought heat to Bob's leg.

The pain was so intense that Bob released his grip on David's throat and screamed as he fell to the floor.

Melody could feel her eyes open wide in a mixture of fear and disbelief at what had just happened.

When she heard Bob's scream, she thought, "I've got to do something!"

She grabbed the phone and dialed the Police.

Speaking into it, she gave them the location and situation, saying, "Please hurry! This is an emergency!"

David rubbed his throat and spoke to Jonathan, "I'm OK, Son. You can let him go now."

Bob was moaning on the living room floor, with slobber coming out of his mouth.

Jonathan looked at his Dad and asked, "Are you sure?"

"Yes," he replied.

"OK, if you say so," Jonathan said as he released his grip.

He looked at his Dad and stated matter-of-factly, "That's how I handle bullies!"

Melody asked, "How did you do that?"

He smiled at his Mom and responded, "I'll tell you later."

Bob was still moaning on the floor, babbling about the pain in his leg, when the Police arrived. They rang the door bell.

David and Melody opened the door and explained to the Officers what had happened, without relating Jonathan's actions.

One of the Policemen pulled both of Bob's hands behind his back, handcuffed him, and lifted him onto his feet, telling him, "You are under arrest for Assault and Disturbing the Peace."

"What is your name?" asked the other Officer, making notes in a small notebook.

"My name is Bob Michaels," he replied sullenly. "That little boy is my Grandson, Jonathan, and the big one is my Son, David."

The same Officer was standing near Bob now and could smell booze on his breath and body.

"Have you been drinking tonight?" he asked.

"I've had a couple of drinks," replied Bob defensively, still slurring the words.

He looked at Jonathan and spoke in an accusing tone, "My Grandson caused me extreme pain in my leg. I fell down on the floor and felt paralyzed for a while!"

The Officer motioned toward Jonathan and said, "You mean this young boy here?"

"Yes!" exclaimed Bob.

The Officer laughed and said, "You have got to be joking! A big strong man like you was taken down by just a boy?"

He motioned to his partner, who began escorting Bob towards the front door.

"Where are we going?" asked Bob, totally befuddled.

The Officer said, "Why, you're going to jail, of course, and your truck will be towed to the impound yard."

He took him out and put him in the back of the Police cruiser.

The Officer taking the notes turned to Melody and asked her for their phone number before he turned to go.

"Thank you for your quick response," she told him.

He touched his hat bill, smiled as he turned, and said, "We are at your service."

He left and got into his patrol car.

David, Melody, and Jonathan stood at the door, watching them drive away.

David put his arms around their shoulders and said, "Let's go back inside. That's enough excitement for one night!"

They all sat down in the living room.

Melody looked astounded at Jonathan and asked again, "How did you do that?"

He looked at his Mom and said, "It is a short story. I was at school. A bully was picking on Petey. When I told him to pick on someone his own size, he started to push me, too. I just grabbed his hand hard and felt the heat going into his hand. It caused him pain in his joints and muscles. I did the same thing to this man when he grabbed Dad's throat, except all I could reach was his leg."

He turned to his Dad and asked, "Was he really my Grandfather?"

David looked at his son and answered, "He says he is, but I've never met him. I'm going to have to call Grandma Julie in the morning and double check. She said he was in Aurora now."

Jonathan said, "Well, he's not a very nice man, whoever he is."

David ruffled his hair and said, "You're a real tiger, you know that?"

Jonathan smiled up at his Dad and responded, "Nobody's going to hurt my Dad and get away with it!"

Melody said, "Well, Tiger, it's time for bed. Off you go!"

"Aw, Mom, do I have to?" he asked.

"You know you do. Don't forget to brush your teeth," she replied. "Remember, even tigers need teeth!"

David smiled to himself as he watched Jonathan go towards his bedroom, thinking, "Who would have guessed it?"

The monitors on Gorbandihar had recorded the whole thing. Miranda reported it to He Who Summons, of course.

He smiled at her and said, "I think We both know that this young man's potential is awesome. Besides, We can't let anybody harm David, now can We?"

He winked at Miranda as she was leaving.

She began smiling to herself over the outcome of this unexpected situation.

CHAPTER 18

The next day, David called Julie and explained everything that had occurred.

"What?" she cried in shock. "Bob actually came there and did that? He said he wanted to see you, but I never dreamed..."

He could hear an audible sob as she ended.

"It's OK, Mom," David said, "It all happened so fast. Melody was very quick to call the Police. He's in jail, but I don't know how long they'll hold him."

"Is Melody and Jonathan all right? I mean, he didn't hurt them, did he?" she asked in a rush of words.

"No, both are just fine," David said.

Then he laughed and said, "Actually, Jonathan took care of Bob in short order. He grabbed his leg and made him hurt so bad that he fell on the floor screaming."

"You mean little Jonathan really took Bob to the floor all by himself?" asked Julie as she smiled at the picture of it.

"He could have done a lot more than that if I hadn't stopped him," replied David. "He was like a tiger when he saw Bob hurting me. He sprang into action just like a big cat."

She replied, "Now that must have been a sight to see!"

Chuckling, he said, "It really was."

He could hear silence on her end of the line.

Finally, she said, "Son, I have some business to handle right now. I'll call you back when I'm finished, OK?"

"Sure, Mom, I have some things to do myself," he responded.

Julie hung up the phone. After checking her address book, she dialed her lawyer and spoke with him at length. She hung up, checked the address for the Aurora Police Station, and picked up her car keys.

When she arrived and parked, she went into the station and spoke to the Desk Sergeant. Shortly, Julie was escorted back to the cell where Bob was incarcerated.

The Policeman noticed that Bob was lying on his bunk, so he used his night club to rattle the bars.

Then he said, "You've got a visitor, Michaels."

Bob sat up on the bunk. When he saw her, he rose to his feet. His appearance was slovenly and disheveled. His face was covered with beard stubble. There was a long moment before recognition registered on his face. When it did, he smiled weakly.

"It's been a long time, Julie. I wouldn't have chosen this location. I wish it had been under different circumstances. What brings you down here?" he asked, trying to smile in what he hoped was a friendly manner.

"That should be obvious, even to you!" she replied coldly. "You told me you wanted to see David and Melody. The least you could have done was make a visit while you were sober! What in the world were you thinking?" she asked angrily, with her face reddening with each word.

He answered, "I was just intent on seeing my son at last. Until I looked up his address, I was unaware that he was married. Also, I didn't know I had a grandson. Believe me, I meant no harm to any of them!"

"Humph!" stated Julie skeptically. "I guess you didn't mean to harm David when you choked him either—in front of Melody and Jonathan at that!"

"Honestly, I just wanted to see them. I sure didn't intend to do it. Choking him was just a reflex action—I got angry during the conversation, and my being drunk did not help any. You have got to believe me—I am so sorry," he said.

She gave him a withering look and said, "That is always what you say after the damage is done, isn't it?"

She continued, "Well, Bob, you wanted a meeting. You've got your wish. I'm here—not because I want to be, but because I think it's necessary. Here's what is going to take place now. You will be served with Restraining Orders which will prohibit you from coming within a certain distance of me, David, and his family."

"Aw, Julie," he said in a pitiful tone. "That's not necessary. I would never hurt you or them!"

She replied, "You already have! You can't be trusted, especially when you're drinking! I've already put in motion everything legally necessary. I've raised David by myself without any help from you! Since we haven't been husband and wife all these years, the Divorce is just a formality. My lawyer will call on you soon with the papers in hand. Whether you sign them or not, the Divorce will proceed through to its conclusion! After that, I'll be done with you for good!"

"Can't we talk about all of this for a few minutes? That's not too much to ask, is it?" he asked pleadingly.

"Before you went to David's house, I was seriously considering having a meeting with you. I left Texas very quickly because I was afraid, both for myself and little David. I did what I thought was best for us at the time. Now, after what you've done, I realize you have not changed a bit, so there's no more to be said! If you sign the papers, that will be good. If you don't, I'll see you in Court. Either way, it's over!" she stated emphatically.

She turned to go.

"It doesn't have to end like this," he said in a sad voice.

She ignored him and walked down the hall to the door leading to the Desk Sergeant's duty station.

She thought as she walked to her car, "I can still feel pity for Bob, simply because he needs help with his Alcoholism. However, my mind is made up! There will be no more harm done to me or my family by him!"

When Julie arrived back home, she dialed David's number. Melody answered the phone.

Julie said, "Hi! Is David there?"

She replied, "Yes, he's here. Please hold on a second, OK?"

Julie could hear her calling his name.

"It's your Mom," she said in the background.

She came back on the phone and said, "Here he is," as she handed him the phone.

"Hi! What's up?" he asked lightly.

Julie replied, "I just went to the Aurora Police Station to speak with your Father. I explained to him that my lawyer will contact him soon with the Divorce papers and Restraining Orders. That will prevent him from coming within a certain distance from you, Jonathan, Melody or me. If he breaks any of the Restraining Orders, he'll go to jail, plain and simple!"

"Do you think that was really necessary?" asked David.

"Yes, it is," she stated quickly. "I left Texas because he knocked me to the floor in one of his drunken binges! I wasn't sure if he would harm you, too, but I wasn't going to stay around to see. Now he was choking you in a drunken rage. He just cannot be trusted!"

She took a deep breath to calm herself and then went on, "I just thought you might like to know what actions I've taken. No one is going to harm my loved ones, especially a drunken, stupid man! I'll let you go for now. I love you guys. Give Jonathan a big hug from Grandma, OK?"

He responded, "Will do. We love you, too, Mom."

As she hung up the phone, he could hear the click.

David thought about the call for a few minutes, but finally shrugged it off and returned to his little family.

CHAPTER 19

Doctor Hollis finished his breakfast and looked in on his son, who was still sleeping. Betty was standing beside him, and he slipped his arm around her waist. He touched his son's forehead, which was warm but not hot to the touch.

He looked at her and cocked his head towards the door. She walked him to the front door. She looked up and stood on tiptoe for her good bye kiss. He laughed and bent his head down to kiss her. She grabbed his head with both hands and returned his kiss.

When he pulled his head up, she said, "Please call me as soon as you get the news on his blood work."

He replied, "I will, Honey, and that's a promise."

She said, "You remember that a promise is not a promise until you keep it?"

He said, "I know. Gotta go."

"Have a nice day at work," she said, smiling pertly at him. "Don't be ogling any of the new nurses now," she teased.

"Right!" he laughed and winked at her before closing the door, heading towards the car.

She thought as she watched him drive away, "I have to use my accumulated vacation time to remain at home to care for Brandon, but I don't mind at all."

Turning towards Brandon's room, she thought, "Caring for him is the most important thing I can do right now."

When Doctor Hollis entered his office, he made a check of his caseload. He went out to the Nurse's Station for coffee and to exchange morning greetings with the staff and fellow doctors. He reviewed his notes, donned a white smock and stethoscope, washed his hands, and quickly finished his coffee.

He thought, "There is something comforting about routine, even in difficult times. I almost always begin my day this way, every day, unless something unusual happens."

He conducted his rounds, checked on his patients, their medical records and their progress. He listened to their complaints, problems, hopes and dreams. He did his best to answer their questions and make small talk, even though his mind was more on his family.

When his rounds were complete, he went to check the lab results on Brandon's blood draw. His hands trembled as he noticed that there was an increased level of white blood cells.

He made a quick call to Doctor Jack Young, who was not only experienced in blood diseases but was a skilled surgeon. He took the lab report and went to consult with him. When he walked up, Doctor Young was speaking to a nurse, giving her instructions for a patient.

He smiled at him and said, "Hello, Dan."

"Hi, Jack. Thanks for taking the time to go over these lab reports with me," he responded.

Jack said, "Let's go in here," as he led the way into an empty hospital room.

Dan handed over the lab reports, which Jack began looking over.

He asked, "Did you have x-rays taken?"

Dan replied, "Oh, yes, of course. They were clear, which ruled out Pneumonia."

"How old is the patient?" he asked as he finished reading the lab report.

"It's our son, Brandon, and he is six years old. We are very concerned because he's been running a fever on and off for three weeks or so. He also has very little appetite," Dan related in a muted voice.

"Does he have any medical records?" Jack asked.

Dan responded, "You know, I'm slipping. I did not bring anything. Of course, he has some medical records. I just didn't think to bring them along. Tell you what, I can go and get them right now."

Jack smiled, put his hand on Dan's shoulder and said, "I'll just have a nurse retrieve them. Once I've checked everything, I'll give you a call so we can discuss it. Will that be OK?"

"Thanks. I'll owe you one," replied Dan.

"Don't worry. I'm glad to help," said Jack with a smile.

Dan walked down the hallway towards the elevators, waving good bye to Jack as he walked.

Later that afternoon, a nurse nodded to Doctor Hollis and handed him a phone.

"Hello," he said.

"This is Jack. Can you please come up here?" he asked.

"Sure," he replied. "I'll be up there as soon as I can get there."

He hung up the phone, told the nurse where he would be, and tapped his pager as he headed for the elevators, not even noticing her nod of understanding.

A couple of minutes later found him on the fourth floor, walking towards Doctor Young's station.

Jack was sitting down at a desk behind the Nurse's Station. When he saw Dan, he rose and walked to meet him. Together, they walked back to the room which they had been in earlier that day.

"I'll be as direct as I can be—there is no other way to say this. It is still too early to be certain, but from the records, symptoms, x-rays, and blood work results, there's a strong possibility that Brandon may have Leukemia. We will need to draw blood again soon to see if the white blood cell count is still increasing and to estimate how fast. If it is, we would follow-up with a bone marrow biopsy, which is very painful as you know."

Dan's face mirrored his concern as he said, "When would we need to do the biopsy?"

Jack replied, "Within a week after the blood draw. We don't want to drag our feet. Time is of the essence, as you know."

Dan shrugged his shoulders in resignation as he said, "Thanks for your frankness. I know how hard it was to do this. Now I have to break this news to Betty. Quite frankly, that weighs heavy on my heart," he stated quietly.

"Would you like my assistance?" asked Jack.

"No, I'll do it, but I'm certainly not looking forward to it," he said.

Dan went back to his station so he could call home.

"Hello," answered Betty. "Who is it?"

"It's me, Honey," he responded. "I just have a few minutes, but I promised I would call you. I'll be as brief as I can. I consulted with Doctor Young and showed him the results of the blood draw. He says it's too early to be certain. We will have to do another blood draw to be positive…"

Before he could say any more, she interrupted him, "Dan Hollis, you level with me right now! What do you suspect?"

"It's possibly Leukemia," he answered softly, struggling to be calm. "I didn't want to tell you this over the phone, but I did promise I would call. I'm sorry, Honey. I really am."

He imagined her face, with the concern on it as well as the shock mirrored there.

Betty struggled to maintain control of her emotions.

Finally, in a tight voice, she said, "Will you come home at the normal time?"

He hesitated and then said, "Well, it will take me about an hour to finish the necessary daily paperwork, so I'll see you in about one and one half hours."

"Good," she said, "because dinner will be ready by then. Brandon has been up and is watching cartoons on television."

"I love you, Betty Hollis. I'll be home as soon as I can," he said as he hung up the phone.

He sat back in his chair and thought, "Dadgummit! I wish I hadn't called, promise or no promise! I should have waited to tell her after I got home. At least I could have been there to console her. I wish I had the power to work a miracle. Wait a minute! Miracle! Of course!"

He sat bolt upright, snapped his fingers, and stated excitedly, "That's it! Now I can't wait to get home!"

CHAPTER 20

David and Melody were having a deep conversation in the living room.

"Mom told me she was having Restraining Orders served on my Father. He will not be allowed within a certain distance from you, me, or Jonathan. Of course, he won't be able to come near her either," he stated.

"It's just as well because he scares me," she responded. "Does that upset you about the Restraining Orders? Mom is just trying to protect us. She wants a Divorce from him anyway, and I can certainly see why."

"Well, I'm just not sure about it all. Alcoholism is a disease, and diseases can be cured. If he were cured, I wonder what kind of a person he would be?" he mused out loud.

Soon afterward, the front door slammed shut, loudly announcing Jonathan's entrance. He bounded into the living room with the non-caring zest of the young. He looked from his Dad to his Mom.

"What's up?" he asked in a mischievous tone.

"Oh, your Mom and I were just having a discussion about your Grandfather," replied David.

"You mean that angry, drunk man, don't you?" Jonathan asked.

"That's not a nice thing to say," corrected Melody. "Also, how many times have I told you to not slam that door?"

"I'm sorry. I just forgot again," he intoned in a soft voice. "You said I should always tell the truth. What I said is true, isn't it, about that man who is supposed to be my Grandpa?"

"Yes, it is," she conceded. "Anyway, he really is your Grandfather."

"Why haven't we seen him before?" he asked in his direct manner.

"Truth is, neither your Mom nor I have an answer to your question. We're as baffled as you are about it. We have just been discussing him and his Alcoholism," volunteered David."

"Besides," said Melody, "we recently found out that your Grandma is having legal papers drawn up and served on your Grandfather very soon. He will be prevented from coming close to any of us or to her in the future. So you won't have to be afraid of him anymore."

Jonathan stuck out his chest defiantly and said, "Oh, he doesn't scare me. If he bothers any of us, I know how to handle him."

She laughed at his posture and the way his little chin jutted out.

When she could finally talk, she said, "You know, I believe you certainly do!"

Jonathan asked, "Dad, when Grandma has those papers served, we won't get a chance to know anything about my Grandpa, will we?"

He replied, "It does look that way. Why would you want to know him, after what happened?"

David and Melody exchanged glances because they had wondered how Jonathan might react to all of these circumstances. Their son's reaction took them by surprise.

"I would just like to find out why he acted like he did, and why he came here anyway. He must have had a reason, don't you think? Can someone be cured from this Alcoholism you say he's got?" Jonathan asked, looking straight into his Dad's eyes.

David thought about it a moment before he answered: "Well, it is a disease so I suppose it can be treated and cured. I've never personally tried to do that, but I believe it could be possible. It's a bad habit as well. One would have to change that person's need for a strong drink to do it."

"I need some answers to my questions. Do you think we could talk to him tomorrow before we can't anymore?" he asked, looking intently at him.

Melody interrupted, "But tomorrow is a school day! Besides, after what he did, I don't want you anywhere near him!"

"It will be OK, you'll see," Jonathan responded soothingly.

Turning to his Dad, he asked, "Can we do that? It won't take very long, and you can square it with my teacher, can't you? It's important to me because he is my Grandpa."

David looked at Melody now, and she came to his rescue.

She said, "I'll tell you what we'll do. You go and get your bath before dinner. Your Dad and I will discuss your request. We will give you an answer before bedtime, fair enough?"

"Yup!" he replied, heading towards the bathroom. "Thanks," he said over his shoulder before closing the bathroom door.

She raised her voice, "Don't forget to wash behind your ears."

Faintly, she heard from behind the closed door, "Aw, Mom!"

She looked intensely at David.

"What are we going to do with him, David?" she asked. "He's more like an adult than a boy. He just has a different way of looking at things."

"Don't worry about it, Sweetheart," he said, smiling. "You know how persistent Jonathan can be, regardless of his age. If he gets something in his mind, he won't give up on it. It would be easier to take care of it now, don't you think? I'll just make a couple of phone calls in the morning to his school and to my work. That would do the trick. I'll drive him to the jail for a quick visit and drop him off at school afterwards."

"You don't think that taking him to see his Grandfather inside a cell will bother him?" she asked, with a concerned look on her face.

"Not really," he replied. "Kids his age are really very resilient with tough situations—we've seen it before."

She said reluctantly, "OK, I guess you are right."

They did small talk at dinner, as usual. Before they put him to bed, they told him their decision.

"Thanks a lot. I need to do this!" he said over his shoulder as he went towards his bedroom.

David and Melody exchanged understanding looks at each other with a smile.

The next morning, while Melody prepared breakfast, David made the necessary phone calls, including a call to the Aurora Police Station to set up a visit for them.

He thought, "That went smoother than I anticipated. My Floor Manager was very supportive and told me to take any time I needed."

They sat down and enjoyed their breakfast. Afterward, Jonathan gave his Mom a hug, and David kissed her good bye at the door.

Jonathan was very quiet as David drove them there. Once inside the building, they were directed to Bob's cell. He was on his feet, awaiting their arrival.

As they approached and stopped outside his cell door, Bob tried to smile as he spoke through the bars, "Hello, again. I would invite both of you in to sit and visit, but you know how it is. This is just not how I imagined it would be."

He then shrugged his shoulders in resignation, dropping his head down towards his chest.

Jonathan stepped forward and asked, "Are you really my Grandfather?"

Bob nodded his head in affirmation, ashamedly.

"Well, you don't act like a Grandfather should act! Grandfathers are kind and friendly. You are mean, and you stink! You look dirty, like you don't bathe. You don't shave or look nice either. I came here to ask you why you choked my Dad!" Jonathan spoke firmly in an accusing tone.

Bob looked at David in bewilderment, as if asking him for help. Finally, he looked at Jonathan, who was looking straight into his eyes intently, waiting for an answer.

Before he could respond, David looked at them and said, "You two will have to excuse me. I have to go use the restroom," as he turned hurriedly to go down the hallway to the Men's Room.

Bob thought, "I have to deflect his questions, so I guess I'd better ask a question of my own."

Aloud, he asked, "How did you cause such pain in my leg?"

"I didn't do anything really. I just grabbed your leg to try to pull you off my Dad," he answered. "Now, are you going to answer my questions? I'm missing school so I could come down here and talk to you because you are my Grandpa."

Bob stuck his hands through the cell bars in a hopeless gesture and said with a catch in his throat, "It's the alcohol, Jonathan. I just can't seem to leave it alone. When I drink it, I feel good for a while, but then I lose control. I know I get mean when I drink. It is just that I can't seem to stop myself."

"Why don't you just quit?" asked Jonathan simply and directly.

"I've tried so many times over the years. It must be obvious to you that I've never been successful," said Bob in quiet resignation as he hung his head again.

Jonathan took a step forward and caught Bob's wrists in his hands. The heat from his hands sent a jolt up Bob's arms like an electrical shock. It traveled up his arms to his shoulders, up his neck and into his brain. He felt a sharp piercing pain inside his head that left as quickly as it had come. The look on his face mirrored pain, shock, and surprise.

When he could find his voice, he croaked, "What just occurred?"

Jonathan released his wrists, stepped back and said. "You'll see, in time."

The incident took place in mere seconds just before David came out of the Men's Room, walking back up to Bob's cell.

The look on Bob's face caused him to ask, "Are you all right?"

He looked at David and said, "What kind of son are you raising? Who is he? I mean, is he a normal human being or not?"

David looked puzzled and asked, "What in the world are you talking about anyway? A better son absolutely could not be found!"

"Well, he just grabbed my wrists and sent a sharp pain clear up to my head! There for a minute, I thought it was going to explode! What happened to me?" he asked.

David turned to Jonathan and asked, "What did you do to him?"

Jonathan looked up at him, responding innocently with a wink Bob could not see, "Nothing at all. I was just talking to him, asking him the questions I needed, and he answered me."

"He's not telling you the truth," Bob stated. "Just now he made a pain go clear up my arms and into my head! The other night, when he grabbed my leg at your house, the pain was unbearable. I know I was intoxicated, but I will never forget it! I'm just curious about how he could do such a thing! After all, he's just a little boy, right?" he finished in disbelief.

"I do know he is my son and your grandson," replied David. "He wanted to talk with you today in person. Now I have to get him to school."

Bob looked at Jonathan for a moment and said, "I don't know why you caused me pain, but I'm still glad for the chance to see you again."

"I'm glad, too. Thank you for answering my questions. It was important to me, and maybe to you," said Jonathan with a smile as he turned with his Dad to walk towards the door.

Once they were in the car and moving along, David asked Jonathan, "Will you please tell me what you did to him?"

"I just made him a better man. He said he choked you because of alcohol, and he couldn't stop drinking. Now he won't be able to drink anymore because I just planted the idea of how bitter it tastes in his mind. He will have to spit it out," he replied with a smile.

"Do you think that will work?" asked David.

"I think it's worth a try. Don't you agree? Only time will tell. But if it does, it just might change him a lot. After all, he is your Father and my Grandpa. I can't wait to tell Grandma Julie all about it!" he exclaimed.

David smiled as he dropped Jonathan off at school.

He thought, shaking his head, "He is our son, but I am amazed at this display of his ability to arrive at a course of action with such sound logic. To say I am proud of him would be an understatement!"

Of course, there were two other beings far away, watching the monitor screens. As they observed Jonathan's decisive actions, they smiled at each other.

Miranda said, "Told you he was amazing, didn't I?"

He Who Summons just laughed.

CHAPTER 21

Dan thought as he drove home, "I think it would be better if I wait until after dinner to talk with Betty. I don't want to spring it on her when I walk through the door."

They had finished dinner and were sitting in the living room, enjoying being with each other in the peaceful quiet of their home.

"Honey, I have an idea to share with you. I want to contact David Michaels and his son, Jonathan. I truly believe that either one of them can heal Brandon if we can get them to help," he stated. "I just wanted to see how you feel about it."

"I think that would be a great idea, but do you really think they will?" she asked.

"I've got a hunch about both of them," he replied. "Call it just a gut feeling, but there's always been something that I cannot explain. We both sensed it since those three incidents that occurred a few years ago, remember?"

Her face brightened into a smile and said, "Oh, I hope you're right. I would do almost anything if it would help our son. After all, what do we have to lose if they refuse?"

He looked at her, smiled, and said, "In that case, it's all settled. I'll find out their address, and we'll go pay them a visit tomorrow. How about Brandon? Will he be up to the trip? It's very important that he be with us so David and Jonathan can see him."

She replied, "He has been feeling a little better, but we'll have to see how he is in the morning. I understand why it's so important to have him with us. Anyway, there's no way I'm going to trust him to a baby sitter in his current condition."

"You're right, of course," he replied. "If he can't make the trip, I will have to convince them to come here."

She reached over and took his hand in hers, giving it a little tug.

"Come on. Let's get some sleep. We can't do anything until we see how he is doing in the morning," she said.

He smiled and followed her towards the bedroom.

Early the next morning, Betty was in the kitchen putting on a pot of coffee and beginning breakfast. Dan was in the bathroom shaving. She went into Brandon's room. He was still asleep as she checked his pulse and touched his forehead, which was a normal temperature. He appeared to be sleeping peacefully.

She went back into the kitchen, poured herself a cup of coffee, added cream and sugar, and began frying bacon. Dan came up behind her and slid his arms around her.

"Good morning, Sunshine," he said as he kissed her ear. "I see you're cooking my favorite meat."

She laughed at his attentiveness, which she enjoyed.

"Do you want eggs or oatmeal with your bacon and toast?" she asked.

"Oh, I think a pair of eggs over easy would do the trick for me," he said smiling at her.

"Coming right up. Just sit down, and I'll pour you a cup of coffee," she said, smiling back at him.

He sat down and watched her glide around the kitchen, getting breakfast ready.

"No doubt about it," he thought. "I love to watch her moving about. She's as good in the kitchen as she is a nurse."

He sipped his coffee as she placed eggs, toast, and bacon on a plate and set it before him. She got her breakfast and sat down across from him.

"Have you looked in on Brandon yet, Honey?" he asked.

141

She could see the concern in his face and answered, "Yes, Dear, I did—just a few minutes ago while you were shaving. His pulse is good, and his forehead is normal to my touch. He seems to be sleeping peacefully, too. I thought it would be good to let him sleep a little while longer, especially since he's breathing normally."

He finished his breakfast and complimented her: "That was really delicious. Thank you."

She smiled at him.

He said, "It's a great idea to let him sleep. I have to locate David's address. The old one on his hospital records is obsolete because I know he's been married for some years now. I'm going to try to call his mother, Julie Michaels. She'll have his current address. Do you remember her?"

"Oh, yes, I remember her very well. She was a nurse working at Fitzsimons Army Medical Center the last time I heard," she replied.

Dan went into the living room and dialed information. In almost no time, he had jotted down Julie's phone number, which he dialed.

A female voice answered the phone and said, "Hello."

He spoke, "Mrs. Michaels, this is Doctor Hollis from the University of Colorado Hospital. I don't know if you remember me."

"Of course, I remember you," she said. "Is there something wrong?"

"No, not at all," he replied. "Oh, I'm sorry. I forgot my manners. Good morning."

"Well, Good morning to you, Doctor Hollis," she said with a laugh. "What can I do for you?"

"I need a favor. Could you give me David's address and phone number?" he asked. "I need to talk to him. It's very important to Betty and me. I'm sure you remember Nurse Betty. She cared for David when he was hospitalized a few years ago. She and I have been married for several years now."

"Oh, I didn't know, but congratulations to both of you. Yes, I do remember her, too. Of course, I'll give David's information to you. Do you have a pen handy?" she asked.

"Yes, I do. Go ahead," he replied.

Dan copied the address and phone number down, chatted with Julie for a few more minutes, and then hung up the phone.

He did not mention what he wanted with David, and Julie did not pry.

Dan went back into the kitchen and said, "Well, Honey, Julie gave us David's information. By the time our son awakens and has his breakfast, perhaps we'll have found a way to help him."

He returned to the living room, picked up the phone, and dialed David's number.

A female voice answered, "Hello."

"Is this David Michaels' residence?" he asked.

"Yes, it is," she replied. "Do you wish to speak with him?"

"Is this Melody?" he asked.

"Yes, it is. Can I ask who is calling?" she asked in a somewhat tentative-sounding voice.

"Hi! This is Doctor Hollis from the University of Colorado Hospital. You may remember me and my wife, Nurse Betty," he said. "We wanted to talk to David if he's at home, but it needs to be in person since it's a personal matter."

"Oh, Doctor Hollis, of course, I remember both of you," Melody said with delight. "David has gone to work. He won't be home until after four o'clock. You could come to talk with him later this afternoon."

"That would be OK, if you're sure David won't mind," he replied.

"I'm sure he will be as happy as I am to see you," she said with a laugh. "We don't get enough company anyway."

"That's great!" he replied. "So, we'll drop by around five o'clock. We will be bringing our young son, Brandon, with us. Thank you very much."

"We'll look for you at that time," she responded. "I will call David and let him know you're coming."

"We'll see you then," he replied, and hung up the phone.

He walked back into the kitchen where Betty was still sipping her coffee.

Dan told her about the call and said, "I was just so intent on talking with David that I never even thought that he might be working."

"It's no wonder, Dear. You've had a whole lot on your plate lately. Besides, you can't be expected to remember every little detail," she chided, smiling sweetly. "Well, we have some time before we have to leave. I know that there's a whole list of things I need to do around here, and I'll bet you that your list is at least as long as mine. The faucet on the utility tub in the laundry room is still dripping. The front storm door closer needs adjusting. Shall I go on?" she asked teasingly.

"No," he responded. "I'll get started and see if I can't narrow the list a little bit. Who knows, maybe I'll even have enough time to change the oil and filter on the car."

A small yawning sound caught Betty's attention. She looked up. There stood Brandon, rubbing the sleep from his eyes, clad in his pajamas with his hair all tousled. She moved over to him and gave him a warm hug.

"Good morning! How did you sleep?" she asked.

"I slept pretty good," he replied. "I heard you and Dad talking. What is there to eat for breakfast? I'm really hungry!" he said, yawning again.

She thought, "That statement makes me very happy!"

Aloud, she said, "What would you like to have?"

His answer surprised her and tickled her at the same time.

"I'd like a donut with some milk and maybe a little bowl of cereal," he said with a smile.

He looked at his Dad and asked, "Could I help you change the oil and filter? I think I might like doing that because I like cars."

Dan laughed and said, "Yes, you can help me, but first you need to eat your breakfast."

Betty was already placing a big glazed donut and a glass of milk in front of him as he sat down.

Dan looked at the size of the donut and winked at his son.

"Do you think you can handle that big rascal all by yourself?" he said, pointing towards it.

Brandon picked it up and said as he took a huge bite out of it, "It doesn't stand a chance with me. You know how much I like these."

Betty watched the little interchange, smiling happily.

She thought, "This is more like our son."

Dan smiled to himself, thinking, "I can see the relief in her face, which is a good thing."

He also smiled at Brandon and said, "Don't eat everything in the kitchen. You'll be too full to help me with that oil and filter change."

Next, he left to get the tools to repair the leaking faucet.

The day actually went by quickly.

At about 4 o'clock, Dan and Brandon came into the kitchen.

"Dad," asked Brandon, "why do we change the oil in the car? Does it wear out?"

"No, but the oil gets dirty after a while. The filter catches foreign matter such as dirt. It gets clogged up and can no longer keep the oil clean. That's why we have to change them to help protect the engine, so it will last longer," he replied.

"It's not really hard to change the oil and filter—just messy," replied Brandon simply, making a face.

Betty was laughing at his facial expression.

Dan laughed as well and replied, "You know, I think you do like cars, mess and all. Come on. We have to get washed up because we have to leave here very soon."

He winked at Betty as they headed for the bathroom to wash up.

She thought as she looked at their retreating backs, "How good it is to see them together like that."

Then a sobering thought came across her mind, and she prayed, "Dear God, please help us!"

CHAPTER 22

David arrived home and went inside to find Melody in the kitchen.

"Hi, Sweetheart. Thanks for calling me about Doctor Hollis and Betty coming over. I wonder what they want to see me about?" he asked. "It's been a very long time. In fact, I haven't seen them since I left the hospital when I was in that hit-and-run accident as a teenager."

She responded, "I have no idea. It's been the same length of time for me, too, as you will remember. Anyway, I've baked some cookies and made a cake. I understand that they have a young son, too, so he and Jonathan can have milk and cookies."

David reached over and picked up a cookie, taking a bite.

"Uhmmm—they aren't the only ones that like cookies—especially chocolate chip, my favorite. They're great." He spoke over his shoulder, "I'm going to grab a quick shower," as he headed towards the bathroom.

She went to the back door and called Jonathan and Petey, who were playing.

When they were in the kitchen, she gave each of them a warm cookie and said, "Petey, we have company coming very shortly.

Jonathan has to get cleaned up, so you need to run home. You two can play again tomorrow. Tell your Mom hello for me."

"OK, Mrs. Michaels," he said, moving towards the door. "See you later, Jonathan."

"See you, Petey," he responded in a muffled tone as he was greedily munching a cookie.

He thought, "I love chocolate chip cookies, especially Mom's!"

Petey had not been gone five minutes when the door bell rang. Melody shook her head as she went to the front door. She opened the door and saw Julie standing there.

"Hi! Excuse me if I seem a little surprised, but we were expecting Doctor Hollis, his wife, and son," she said.

Julie laughed and said, "I'm sorry. I didn't know you were expecting company, even though I talked to Doctor Hollis just this morning to give him your address and phone number."

Melody replied, "Come on in, and I'll put on some coffee and hot water for tea."

They both went into the kitchen.

David came into the room and hugged Melody.

"Hi, Mom," he said grinning over Melody's shoulder. "You're next, you know."

"You sure smell nice and fresh," Melody said, pulling back and looking David in the eyes.

"I feel that way, my Love," he said as he smiled and gave her another hug.

After he released her, he moved over to give his Mom a warm hug.

"What could be better?" he said, laughing. "I have my two favorite girls here in the kitchen together."

"You're in a good mood, Davey. I understand Doctor Hollis and Betty are coming for a visit. Will I be in the way?" she asked.

"Of course not. Besides, you know them as well as we do," he said.

Jonathan came into the kitchen. When he spotted Julie, he immediately ran over to her so he could get a hug.

"Hi, Grandma! I didn't know you were coming for a visit. Mom baked a bunch of great cookies, if you like chocolate chips," he said as he beamed up at her.

Julie laughed as she hugged him.

"I do like chocolate chip cookies, Jonathan," she said.

Melody stated with a pleased smile, "I also baked a chocolate layer cake."

"OK!" exclaimed Jonathan, excited at the tantalizing thought of a big slice of cake.

Melody anticipated the question that was sure to follow because she could see it in his eyes, so she said, "You can have a slice of cake with a glass of milk later."

Melody laughed because she knew her son and waited for the rejoinder which was also a certainty.

"Aw, Mom," he said.

David laughed, too, at the interplay between his wife and son.

The happy teasing was interrupted by the door bell. David and Melody went to the front door, with Jonathan close behind them.

David opened the door for their expected visitors and said, "Hi! We have not seen you in years!"

Doctor Hollis and Betty said simultaneously, "Hi there!"

Doctor Hollis then said, "It has been a long time, David and Melody. This young man is, of course, Jonathan. My, how he has grown!" Placing a hand on his son's shoulder, he continued, "This is our son, Brandon."

"Won't you come in?" Melody asked courteously.

David ushered them into the living room. Julie was waiting there and moved forward to greet them.

"Hello! It's so good to see you both. Brandon looks like a fine boy," she said.

Jonathan and Brandon took matters into their own hands, as boys will.

Jonathan asked, "Do you like cookies? My Mom makes big chocolate chip cookies."

"I love cookies," replied Brandon. "My favorite is Mom's peanut butter cookies, but I like chocolate chip, too. Can I have one?" he asked unabashedly.

"Brandon," Betty said reprovingly, "we've just got here and already you're mooching a cookie."

Melody said with a laugh, "Why don't we all go into the kitchen? I'll get the boys a cookie and some milk. I have a fresh pot of coffee and hot water for tea." She looked at Jonathan, smiled and said, "I also can serve some chocolate layer cake, if you like."

Both boys said simultaneously, "Wow! That's great!"

Once everyone was seated and refreshments were served, everyone settled in.

154

While they were talking, Doctor Hollis said, "Would you all please call me Dan? It just sounds too formal to keep calling me Doctor Hollis."

They responded simultaneously, "You bet!"

Jonathan looked at Brandon and asked, "Would you like to see some of my toys? Mom, can Brandon and I go play in the back yard for a little while?"

Melody nodded her head, and both boys scooted for the back door.

Dan looked in relief as the boys left, thinking, "My task will be much easier without the boys' presence."

He said aloud, "Betty and I really appreciate you seeing us like this on such short notice."

Betty nodded and smiled at them.

Dan continued, "I really don't know where to begin, and this is awkward for us. We just got the news from a consulting doctor, which I agree with, that Brandon has Leukemia. He displays all the symptoms now, and his blood work reveals an elevated level of white blood cells. That doctor wants to do more blood work soon and a bone marrow biopsy, which is extremely painful for the patient, within a week after the blood draw!"

He stopped as his voice caught in his throat, overcome with emotion.

When he could continue, he said, "What we have to ask is a little bit strange," as he cast a furtive look at Julie.

David caught on quickly and said, "It's OK to talk in front of my Mom."

Dan struggled with his thoughts, but finally continued, "Well, I'll just get to the point. Betty and I talked it over and decided to see you to ask for your help. We believe that, somehow, you and Jonathan have special powers to heal in a way that regular doctors, such as myself, are unable to do."

Betty's eyes were filled with tears as she spoke softly, "I saw you heal yourself in the hospital all those years ago when you regained consciousness. We strongly believe you also healed Melody of both Polio and Pneumonia—you were in the room next door. You pretended innocence all the while, but the evidence was clear. We both saw Jonathan heal Petey in the Emergency Room when he fell. Well, we thought that, since you have a little son, too, you might understand how we feel, and you would heal our son. We will pay you whatever you want to charge."

She stopped, unable to go on, with tears now falling freely down her face.

Melody's eyes were also full of tears as she reached over to comfort Betty.

Julie's eyes were tearing up as she thought of David healing her Cancer as well.

David thought about his own son, with his mind flooded with memories.

He thought, "I realize that, if I do this healing, it will give away both our secrets. What would He Who Summons and Miranda do about that? Will they diminish my powers or Jonathan's? I've already experienced problems years ago when I was greedy and made gold. But since Jonathan's was a genetic transfer, what could change? So much to think about—it's almost overwhelming!"

He looked at the agony in their faces and thought, "I know that I alone must reach this decision. A little boy's life hangs in the balance. Without my help, he will surely not make it. Existing technology is just not good enough! I could heal Brandon, even if I have to lose my power. But I need time to think in order to make this decision."

Aloud, he said, "First of all, if I could do what you ask from me, I wouldn't charge a penny for it. Let's say that I do have these powers, and I can heal Brandon. My privacy and secrets would cease to exist, and so would Jonathan's. How would this affect my family and our future?"

Dan responded, "You won't have to worry about that because Betty and I will swear not to say a word. Just think for a minute. We could have let the secret out when we suspected you had powers at the hospital years ago. It's been many years ago now, and it has been safe with us all this time."

"That is true," David admitted, "but there are other ramifications involved—serious ones which I cannot explain. I need some time to consider everything. I'll tell you what—give me a day or so to think about this. I'll call to let you know what I decide. Is that fair enough?"

Dan made eye contact with Betty, who nodded at him.

"That's more than fair," Dan said. "At least, you didn't just say no. After all, we are requesting a lot from you, but we ask because it means so much to us, and it means even more to Brandon. We're in the same business of healing, but this time, healing is well beyond any known medical capability."

Dan and Betty rose to go.

Melody called the boys in from their play and said, "They have to leave, Jonathan, so you can say good bye to Brandon for now."

Jonathan looked up at Brandon's parents and asked, "Will you bring Brandon back so we can play together some more?"

Dan and Betty exchanged a look.

Finally, Dan responded, "We'll see," as he gave David an imploring look.

David and Melody walked with them to the front door. The boys were already on the porch, jabbering away.

"I have given my word that I'll call you," David told Dan as they shook hands. "In the meantime, don't set up the additional blood work or the bone marrow biopsy. I understand that time is vital."

"All right. That's good enough for us!" exclaimed Dan.

After they had left, everyone was in the kitchen.

Jonathan thought, "I wonder if I could finagle another piece of chocolate cake before dinner?"

Aloud, he said, "What's wrong with Brandon anyway, Dad? He seems really weak, and he doesn't have a good skin color. He actually had a hard time playing with my truck. He wasn't even strong enough to push it! Honestly, I almost touched him to see if I could help, but I wanted to talk with you about it first."

"It's good that you thought that. He has a problem with his blood, and it's very serious," he responded.

Julie asked, "What would happen if you helped him? You mentioned some serious ramifications. Maybe I should be asking if you can do it?"

"Healing him isn't the problem," he replied. "If I do this, I've broken my promise to He Who Summons and Miranda because I was not supposed to tell about my ability. No one was to know about us or what we can do. That's the problem. I am afraid of the consequences," he said.

"I see," she responded, "so it really is a dilemma, isn't it?"

David was sitting at the kitchen table, and Jonathan went over to stand beside him.

He put his arm around his Dad's shoulders and said, "It'll be OK. He Who Summons and Miranda will understand. They're really nice. Just you wait and see."

David smiled at his son, patted his hand, and replied, "You're probably right. Anyway, can we enjoy another slice of your Mom's chocolate cake?" he asked as he winked at Melody, who was about to object.

"Yup!" yelped Jonathan in delight.

CHAPTER 23

He Who Summons moved His hands over His console to summon Miranda. He then requested some Native elixir. Shortly, a lady carried in a tray containing glasses and a tall container. She set it on the table beside Him.

"Thank you, Lou Anne," He said softly.

She nodded towards Him with a big smile as she left through an entry way.

His eyes were closed in contemplation, sitting in His favorite chair, when He heard Miranda's familiar voice, saying, "You summoned me, Master?"

"Ah, yes," He said, opening His eyes. "Did you observe the meeting between David, Doctor Dan Hollis, and his mate, Betty?"

"I did," she answered. "It must truly be very difficult for David. He's torn between healing and doing what he promised to Us."

"What did you think about Doctor Hollis?" He asked. "You already know it's true that they cannot heal this disease."

Miranda thought for a few seconds and said, "This doctor is the same one who was taking care of David in the University of Colorado Hospital. Betty, as you know, is a highly trained nurse. As far as I understand, both of them are hard working and very capable according to their level of knowledge. As we have observed so often, you know there are many diseases they cannot cure."

He Who Summons responded, "That is exactly the reason why we brought David here: To learn how to heal these diseases among humans. The Earthlings are the most advanced species in all our galaxies. They have such a great potential, if they will just awaken to it and use their inherent abilities! It seems to take them a very long time to accept new ideas. That's why it requires so much patience on Our part."

She stated, "I understand, Master. I was watching young Jonathan console his Dad. I must admit, I was touched. I was also gratified because he thought We were really nice. He shows so much wisdom, understanding, and promise for one so young."

"I agree completely," He replied. "What do you think David will decide to do? We both know that human choices are not mandated by anyone outside of that person."

Miranda gazed intently at He Who Summons and replied, "I hope he does what We taught him to do, which is to use his powers to heal Brandon."

"I believe you're beginning to think like Me," He said, laughing. "I'll be very disappointed if he doesn't heal him."

She smiled and responded, "If I think like You, it's because I've worked with You for so long."

He smiled in return and stated, "Dan and Betty just might be very good candidates for Our Training Program. What do you think about that as a solution? If David does choose to heal Brandon, We could bring Dan here for training and her afterward. Both of them would of course be required to maintain secrecy, and this in turn would cover David's secret."

She spoke, "I'm always amazed at Your depth and clarity of wisdom. It seems that You can always solve a problem by coming up with a new solution. I think that, indeed, would solve David's quandary. You've wanted to train more humans so they can heal as well. This would be an ideal way to resolve both problems!"

He said, "You know, even though he's been sworn to secrecy, his healing of Brandon would justify Our belief in him."

He Who Summons poured Each of Them some elixir.

When He had taken a big sip, He asked, "How did your young ones like Jonathan?"

She answered, smiling, "They enjoyed him quite a bit. They are far advanced over him, but he did just fine. Jonathan was very surprised at the difference in the toys up here."

"Good," He responded. "You know they are very easy to like—David, Melody and Jonathan. I'll be watching closely to see what David's decision will be. It's going to be very interesting. It could positively change more lives than he thinks."

"I'll be observing it, too, Master. Was there another reason You summoned me?" she asked.

"None whatsoever," He answered with a smile. "I just wanted to get your opinion on Our young friends from Planet Earth. They are very complicated, and their power of choice certainly causes them a lot of angst."

She rose, nodded, and said, "It is most fascinating to see how humans go about solving their problems. I'm sure David will make the right decision because, as a dad, he's experienced the same emotions as Dan and Betty."

She moved towards the entry way as she said lightly, "Well, it's back to work for me."

Once again, He closed His eyes in contemplation, with a smile on His face.

CHAPTER 24

Harvey Tuckerson, Julie's lawyer, was parked in the Aurora Police Station parking lot. He stubbed out his cigarette in the ash tray, reached over to the passenger side to retrieve his briefcase, and got out. He locked his car door and briskly walked through the front door.

Harvey had been to this Police Station many times in the past. He knew many of the Policemen and all of the Desk Sergeants by name. Today, the Desk Sergeant on duty was Carl Jamison, whom Harvey had known for years.

"Hello, Carl," he said. "How are you doing? Is the family well?"

"Oh, hi, Harvey. I'm doing as well as can be expected—just getting older and grayer," he said with a laugh. "The family is just fine. I do get real antsy sometimes because I'm riding this desk instead of a patrol cruiser."

Harvey laughed along with him and asked, "Do you have an inmate named Bob Michaels here?"

"Why, yes, I do," Carl answered. "Actually, we've had him for a couple of days now. Seems he got aggressive and assaulted one of our citizens, who just happened to be his son, no less!"

"Well, that's why I'm here. I wonder if I could see him for a few minutes?" he asked.

Carl responded, "Sure, you can."

He motioned for a young Officer to come over and gave him brief instructions.

Carl looked at Harvey and said, "Officer Taylor will take you back to Bob's cell."

"Thanks a lot," he said with a smile. "I won't be too long."

That Officer escorted him to the cell and said, "Do you need a chair? Do you want me to wait?"

He looked at him, grinned, and said, "Yes, that would be good. No, all I have is some papers to discuss with him. He can't get out, and I can't get in, so I believe we're OK."

The Officer gave him a look that would fry an egg as he left.

Harvey thought, "Young Police Officers are dangerous—they all need time to learn and mature. He'll lose that self-important attitude in no time—he just has a new badge, that's all."

The Officer quickly returned with a chair and then left. Harvey sat down.

He looked at the man in the cell and thought, "He is sitting dejectedly on his bed. He's unkempt, needs a shave, and his eyes have dark rings under them."

Aloud, he said, "Are you Bob Michaels?"

Bob answered harshly, "Yes, that's me. Who are you? I don't know you."

"My name is Harvey Tuckerson," he said, "and I'm a lawyer representing Mrs. Julie Michaels, your wife. I just might be able to help you while I'm doing that. I have the Divorce papers here. If you sign them, I'll talk with Julie and David about dropping the Disturbing the Peace and Assault Charges against you. What do you think? It'll save you a Court case, lawyer's fees, and could work out very good for both you and Julie. If this Divorce goes to Court, you know the Judge will rule in her favor—especially in light of what just happened at David's house."

Harvey noticed Bob's expression was already showing anger so he thought, "I'm not going to mention the Restraining Orders. Carl or one of the other Desk Sergeants will serve them on him before he's released."

When Bob made no effort to respond, he rose from the chair, snapped his briefcase closed, looked at him and said, "Just think about my offer because I believe it'll save you both time and money. Don't think too long, though, because I am prepared to file these papers shortly, either with or without your signatures."

He turned to leave.

Bob finally spoke, "Wait just a minute. If they drop the charges, will I be released right away?"

"Yes," he replied, "because they won't have any reason to hold you anymore."

Bob said hesitantly, "Give me a minute to think, will you?"

Harvey sat back down and gave him a stern look.

Bob thought, "When Julie came to visit me, my hope for reconciliation with her died. I need to get out of here so I can clean myself up and get back to work. I need to prove that I can be a good man and not just a mean drunk!"

Aloud, he said with a sigh, "OK, I'll sign the papers, but I want your promise that you'll talk to them about dropping the charges. You might not believe me, but I never meant to harm anyone."

Harvey kept his face grim, pulled out the papers, and showed Bob where to sign.

After he had the signatures on the required copies, he said, "I'll talk to Julie and David shortly. I wish you luck, Mr. Michaels."

He thought as he looked at the grungy man in front of him, "You are going to need it!"

He put the papers into his briefcase, rose from the chair again, turned on his heel, and walked down the hallway.

When he was back in the front, he pulled out the Restraining Orders and handed them to Carl, who proceeded to look them over.

"Say, can I use a phone? I need to make a couple of calls," he said.

Carl replied, "Sure, use that one over there at the other desk," as he motioned towards the phone with his thumb.

"Thanks," Harvey muttered as he opened his briefcase to retrieve his phone book.

Once he located Julie's number, he dialed it and waited. She answered the call on the first ring. Without hesitation, he launched into the details of his visit with Bob, being as brief as possible.

"Oh!" she gasped. "He signed the papers? That's wonderful! Was he served the Restraining Orders?"

He explained, "Not yet—those will be served by the Desk Sergeant before he is released. I thought it would be better to get the Divorce papers signed first."

"That was a smart move," she said, "because he has quite a temper. I wouldn't have thought about that."

"That's how I earn my pay, Mrs. Michaels," he said with a laugh.

"I won't be Michaels much longer," Julie said exuberantly.

"I told Bob that I'd talk with you and David about dropping all the charges. It will save him time and money for Court, lawyer's fees, and fines. He won't be able to bother any of you, anyway, with the Restraining Orders in force," he said patiently.

"It's OK by me. Let me give you David's phone number so you can call him directly," she said. "You'll be far more persuasive than I can be."

"Sure, just give it to me, and I'll give it a shot," he replied.

She did so.

He stated, "As soon as I talk with David, I'm going to take these Divorce papers to the Court and file them for you."

"That's wonderful!" she exclaimed with a heavy sigh. "I can hardly believe that it all went so smoothly, and it will be over soon."

"Sometimes it happens that way," he replied. "I just wanted to let you know the good news. I'll ring off for now because I want to make that call to David."

"OK," she said. "Talk to you later. Thank you so very much. This takes a big weight off my mind. Bye!"

Harvey heard the phone click.

He turned to Carl and asked, "If David Michaels drops the charges against his Father, can he do it by phone?"

Carl replied, "No, he'll have to come down here with some identification and sign the forms to drop them."

"Gotcha," he replied as he dialed David's number.

Melody answered the phone. He briefly explained who he was and that he needed to talk with David personally.

"David's still at work, Mr. Tuckerson," she responded. "I can give you his work number if you like."

"That would be good," he replied. "If you have it handy, I have pen and paper ready."

She gave it to him.

"Thank you. Have a good day," he said and hung up the phone.

He smiled at Carl as he dialed David's number and quipped, "What did we ever do before telephones?"

A man's voice answered the phone.

Harvey asked, "Is this David Michaels?"

"Just a moment," the deep voice said.

A moment later, another man's much gentler voice said, "You asked for me, so how can I help you?"

Harvey explained who he was and what he was calling about as thoroughly as he could, while trying to keep it as brief as possible at the same time.

David listened intently and, when Harvey finished telling his story, he responded, "You mean he signed the Divorce papers, just like that?"

"That's about it," he replied. "When we finish this conversation, I'll drop by the Courthouse and file them. After that, it will be a mere formality for the Judge to apply his signature. If you agree to drop all the charges against Bob, the Police will release him from custody. When he leaves the Police Station, the Desk Sergeant will serve him with the Restraining Orders. He won't be able to harm either your family or your Mom anymore, but he will be able to work so he can make his living. What do you say?"

David thought for a few seconds and replied, "What do I have to do? Can I get him released with a phone call?"

"No," he responded, "you'll have to go to the Aurora Police Station and show your identification to the Desk Sergeant. He will get forms for you to sign to drop the charges."

"OK," David said, "I'll stop by on my way home and do that. You know, I don't really believe my Father is a bad person. He just needs help with his drinking problem. Thanks for calling me and giving me the good news about my Mom."

"No problem. I was glad to help," replied Harvey as he hung up the phone and turned to Carl.

"David is going to stop by here today on his way home from work," he said. "He'll sign the forms to drop all the charges against his Father. Do you think I can see Bob again for another minute or so?"

"Sure," replied Carl. "Go ahead back there—you know the way," he said with a laugh.

Harvey made his way back to Bob's cell to give him the good news.

Bob looked relieved and said, "Thanks for helping me."

He replied, "Well, you are lucky because, after what you did, I'm not sure many people would be so forgiving."

"I think so, too," Bob responded with a grateful look.

Harvey thought, "Well, he might be all right now, but he doesn't know about the Restraining Orders yet, which is just as well."

He turned on his heel, left the building, and proceeded to keep his word about filing the papers at the Courthouse.

CHAPTER 25

After work, David went in to sign the necessary forms at the Aurora Police Station to drop the charges.

He thought, "I don't want to go back to see my Father because I don't begin to know what to say to the man. Frankly, putting him behind bars in the first place was a little too drastic. After all, there's no way he could ever really hurt me, Jonathan, or Melody—not with the powers we possess at our disposal. Maybe he will seek help for his drinking problem. Jonathan is absolutely sure his Grandfather will never drink again. Time will tell. Right now, I have to take care of more pressing matters."

He did what he came there to do, turned on his heel, and left quickly.

As he was driving home, he thought, "I need to settle this question about helping little Brandon. I am wrestling with my secrecy problem and my promise to He Who Summons and Miranda. But he has been occupying almost all of my thought processes. How could I possibly not help him? Well, it's simple—I just can't. I'll heal him, and let the chips fall where they may! My compassion will not let me do otherwise. After all, They taught me this. Perhaps They will understand, but if that doesn't happen, I will have to face the consequences! At least, that little boy would enjoy a full life!"

With that decision made, a wonderful calmness came over him. A smile came to his lips as he was flooded with the certainty of knowing that he had made the right decision.

David arrived at home and went inside to the kitchen. He put his arms around Melody, gave her a huge hug, and kissed her passionately. She laughed, and so did he.

"Why are you in such a good mood, husband of mine?" she asked, catching her breath.

He responded, "For one thing, I went by the Police Station on the way home and signed the release papers to drop the charges against my Father."

With alarmed concern in her face and voice, she stepped back from him and stated, "I knew Mr. Tuckerson needed to talk with you, but I never thought about that as a possibility! What will happen if he decides to come around here again?"

"Before he's released, the Desk Sergeant will serve him with the Restraining Orders, which are Court Orders signed by a Judge. He will be prohibited from coming near us or Mom. If he dares to do such a thing, he will go straight back to jail," he said.

Jonathan came in from playing at Petey's house.

"Hi, Dad," he said as he went over and hugged him. "What's going on, anyway?"

David looked at his son, who had the uncanny knack of coming right to the point.

"Oh, nothing really. I was just explaining to your Mom how I signed the necessary forms to let your Grandpa out of jail. She's concerned he will try to harm us again, but I don't think that will happen."

Jonathan stuck out his chest and said, "Grandpa won't drink anymore because I fixed him," he said proudly. "I think that he's only mean when he drinks."

"What did you do to him?" asked Melody. "How could you stop him from drinking?"

"Well, I put the thought into his brain that alcohol tastes really bad, and he won't be able to swallow it," replied Jonathan matter-of-factly.

David smiled and said, "I hope that it works, Jonathan. If it does, it will help him for the rest of his life."

He continued, "Anyway, sit down here at the table with us. I want to share something even more important with you and your Mom. I've given a lot of thought to healing Brandon. I've reached a decision."

Both Melody and Jonathan leaned forward anxiously in their chairs, watching David expectantly.

"I've decided to go ahead and help that little boy. Healing is what I've been taught, and it's what I plan to do," he said with quiet finality.

"Yippee!" yelled Jonathan, jumping excitedly out of his chair and hopping around the room. "That's great, Dad!"

"That's wonderful, Darling. I know Dan and Betty will be so happy. When are you going to let them know?" she asked.

"Right now is as good a time as any," he said as he was reaching for the phone to dial them.

The phone rang several times. David had a sinking feeling that no one was home. Finally, a woman's voice answered. He recognized Betty's voice.

"Hello, Betty. This is David. How are you, and how is Brandon?" he asked.

"Oh, I'm doing all right under the circumstances. He is holding his own for now," she responded with a catch in her voice.

"I just called to give you some good news. I've decided to heal Brandon," he said gently.

There was a long silence on the other end of the phone, but he could hear her sobbing uncontrollably.

Slowly, she regained her composure and asked in a strained voice, "When can you do it?"

"That is what I called to set up. We can come over to your house, or you can come over here. Is Dan at home, or is he working?" asked David.

"He's here. If you can wait for a moment, I'll get him. He's actually in the back yard," she said.

David waited until Dan's voice came on the phone.

"Betty says you've decided to heal Brandon. When? Where?" he asked excitedly.

David answered, "Whenever and wherever it's convenient for you."

"How about in the next thirty minutes? That's about how long it will take us to get to your house!" Dan exclaimed.

"If that works for you, it'll be just fine for us. We'll be waiting for you," David said.

Dan finished the conversation by saying, "I can't begin to tell you how much we appreciate this! We'll be there as soon as we can."

"OK," replied David, "so we'll see you shortly," and he hung up the phone.

David and Melody waited, sitting at the kitchen table and enjoying milk and a cup of hot tea, respectively.

Jonathan was in the living room, watching television when the door bell rang.

"I'll get it," hollered Jonathan as he opened the front door.

Dan and Betty stood there with Brandon, who was peeking out from behind his dad.

"Hi!" he said with a big smile. "Come on in. Mom and Dad are in the kitchen."

"We were in the kitchen, Jonathan," said David, laughing as he stepped up behind his son.

David extended his right hand towards Dan, who promptly extended his own in a firm hand shake.

"You folks come on in and make yourselves at home," said David with a warm smile as well.

Melody said, "You boys go watch the television. The rest of us will go into the kitchen. We were just having milk and a cup of hot tea. Would you like some, or perhaps some fresh coffee?"

When everyone was seated at the table with their chosen beverage, David smiled and said, "I want to mention a couple of things before I begin. First of all, both of you know that I can heal—and so can Jonathan to a lesser degree—but he's getting stronger every day. You know that you all must maintain our secrecy."

Dan cleared his throat and said, "We've given our word that we will never betray either you or Jonathan. We'll also stress to Brandon that he is to tell no one—not a word. More than that, I don't know what else I can say to convince you that we are sincere."

Betty was nodding her head in assent.

"I believe you both. That's why I've agreed to do this. I want to make a suggestion, however. I want to see what you both think of what I'm going to say. When you run into a medical problem that you can't cure, you could call me in. I could undertake the healing. You two could take the credit. What do you think about my idea?" quizzed David.

"That sounds good, but, like you, we would like to think it over so we could discuss your idea between us," responded Dan.

"Touché!" David said, with a laugh. "Come on. Let's get Brandon into Jonathan's bedroom so we can get him healed."

Dan took Betty's hand and followed David, who had his arm around Melody. They went into Jonathan's room as David called the boys to stop watching television and come into the bedroom. Melody went to the windows to pull the drapes closed to maintain their privacy. Dan lifted Brandon onto Jonathan's bed.

"What else can I do? Does he need to have his clothes and shoes removed?" he asked.

"No," said David with a smile. "He's fine like he is. Brandon, I want you to lay still and close your eyes. What I do next will not hurt you at all, I promise. You may feel some heat coming from my hands. Are you ready?"

Brandon nodded his head.

Jonathan took his hand and said, "I'll be right here by your side."

"OK," Brandon replied.

"Now close your eyes, and I'll get started," said David.

Brandon closed his eyes, but before David could begin, a bright light appeared. Miranda had entered the room through the bedroom wall, wearing her white gown and golden girdle.

Jonathan said with excitement, "Hello, Miranda! It's great to see you again!"

Both Dan and Betty's faces showed shock and surprise.

"Hi, Miranda," said David. "This is Doctor Dan Hollis and his wife, Betty. This is their son, Brandon, who has been diagnosed with Leukemia. I was just getting ready to heal him."

Brandon opened his eyes, saw the beautiful lady, and asked her in wonder, "Are you an angel?"

Miranda answered as she laughed, "No, I'm not an angel, Brandon. As you can see, I don't have any wings."

She turned so he could see her back.

Miranda nodded to Dan and Betty and said, "I'm pleased to meet both of you. We've been watching you for some time now. My name is Miranda, and I'm from Gorbandihar. He Who Summons has sent me here on a mission. David, can I assist you with Brandon?" she asked.

"No, I think you've trained me well enough so I can handle this job," David said with a short-lived smile. "But what is your mission this time? Let me guess. You've come to tell me the consequences of my decision, right?" he asked anxiously.

"We'll talk about my mission after you are done. Go ahead with your healing, David," replied Miranda with a disarming smile.

David's thoughts were so intense that he did not really notice her smile. He looked at her resignedly for a moment.

He turned to Brandon and said dispiritedly, "OK, guy, close your eyes again. Hopefully, I'll get the job done this time."

Brandon did as he was told, and David began moving his hands from head to toe, approximately one to two inches above the boy's body.

Dan thought excitedly, "I think I can actually feel heat coming from David's hands! Fascinating!"

He looked at Betty, who also had a look of wonderment on her face.

Just as suddenly as it had begun, it was finished.

David said, "Brandon, you can open your eyes now. How do you feel?" he asked.

Brandon sat up and said, "I feel great! Can I go play with Jonathan now?"

"Sure, go ahead. You two can go play in the back yard," David said with a laugh.

David looked at Melody and said, "Sweetheart, let's have some refreshments for our guests. Come on. Let's go back into the kitchen so we can be more comfortable."

Dan thought, "Events are moving just a little too fast for me! Who is Miranda? Where is this Gorbandihar?"

Aloud, Dan asked, "Is Brandon actually healed now, David—just like that?"

"To answer your question," responded David, "yes, he's OK. I know you two must have dozens of questions, so let me start with an explanation. First of all, Miranda comes from a Planet called Gorbandihar. Yes, she did just come through the bedroom wall. She is very far advanced over humankind. She is the one who taught me how to heal. In fact, Melody and Jonathan have also been to her Planet."

Dan looked at Miranda and said, "My son thought you were an angel, and I can see why. How do you teach a human like David to heal?"

Miranda smiled and said, "I thought you would ask that question."

With that, she moved her hands over Dan's head, and a glowing golden crescent appeared, which startled both him and Betty. Next, Miranda moved her hands over Betty's head, and another one appeared. Miranda put her hands up to her own head, and a third one appeared there.

She continued, saying, "I don't have our technology or screens with me, but I believe I can give you a small sample of what we teach. The objects above your heads help by stimulating your brain to receive, understand, and retain complex information. Now I won't speak, but my thoughts will communicate a sample of this process. Are both of you ready to give it a try?"

Dan and Betty both nodded, with their eyes wide open in wonder.

Miranda used her crescent to send mental images and names of the human anatomy to their crescents. Dan and Betty looked at each other and smiled in recognition as the information came into their minds. In a few minutes, Miranda stopped sending and moved her hands, first over Betty's head and then Dan's, causing the crescents to vanish. After that, she raised her hands above her own head, causing it, too, to vanish.

187

Miranda smiled as she asked, "If I asked you questions about the anatomy that we've just gone over, could you answer the questions correctly?"

"Yes, I could. However, it is somewhat different from what I currently know," replied Dan.

"I agree," responded Betty.

"Good," replied Miranda, "because I was sent by He Who Summons to make both of you an offer. Would you come to Gorbandihar so you could learn to heal like David? However, because you have your son to take care of, it would be best if only one of you came at a time."

At that moment and before they could answer, Jonathan and Brandon burst into the house.

"Mom, can Brandon and I have a cookie and a glass of milk?" asked Jonathan.

Melody laughed and said, "Please excuse the boys for interrupting," as she smiled at Miranda.

She looked at Jonathan and told him, "The cookies are in the cookie jar. You may get one for Brandon and yourself while I pour both of you a glass of milk. Oh, and please put the cookie canister on the table so we adults can enjoy one, too."

Dan looked at Betty and said with a smile, "You know, a cookie would be very nice."

He took one and gave Betty one. Next, he held the canister out towards Miranda, who shook her head.

"No, thank you," she said with a smile.

Brandon walked over to Miranda, looked deeply into her eyes, and asked, "Are you sure you're not an angel? You look like one to me!"

Miranda smiled at him and replied, "No, Brandon. I still don't have wings, but I can do a few neat things. Jonathan, please throw that ball over there to me."

Jonathan promptly threw the ball to her, which she deftly caught. She moved her hands over the ball, and it began to glow, turning many iridescent colors.

"Oh, boy, a sparkle ball!" yelped Jonathan in delight. "Can we can play with it?" he asked.

For an answer, she flipped the ball to him, who in turn tossed it over to Brandon. He stood silently looking at the beautiful changing colors, his eyes shining with wonderment.

"It's so pretty," he said softly.

Miranda smiled and said, "Young ones are the same on our Planet."

"Do you have children?" asked Betty.

Miranda nodded her head in assent, looked at Jonathan, and asked, "Do you remember their names?"

He stepped forward, thrust his chest out, and said importantly, "Miranda has eight young ones. From the oldest to the youngest, they are: Eroc, thirty years old; Roan, twenty years old; Latox, eighteen years old; Jakin, fifteen years old; Elo, thirteen years old; Notan, twelve years old; Rendy, ten years old; and last but not least, there is Breta, who is eight years old. You see, Miranda, I didn't forget their names or their ages. Do you want me to tell them how old you are?"

David looked at his son and said, "Telling a lady's age isn't a very nice thing to do."

"I do not mind. Go ahead, you may tell them," said Miranda, smiling.

"She is one hundred and sixty-one years old!" Jonathan stated importantly.

Dan and Betty's mouths dropped open in complete astonishment.

"Actually, I'm just becoming middle aged," stated Miranda, still smiling.

Dan looked at her and said, "Unbelievable! What can I say? As to your amazing offer, I know Betty is as thrilled as I am. We just need to talk about it so we can plan a time when each of us can come to Gorbandihar. How long would we be gone, Earth time? When we do get our plans made, how can we contact you?"

She responded, "It will take each of you at least a week for the training, depending on your absorption rate. You both already have a good medical background, so that will help. Once you are ready to set it up, just tell David. He will be able to contact me when the time is right."

"That will work out just great," said Dan, "but now we must be getting home."

"Of course, I understand," she replied. "In the meantime, should you have any questions about the trip itself, just talk to David and Melody. They can fill you in as to how it works for your bodies. You see, only your spirits will make the trip to Gorbandihar."

"Oh, I see," he said quietly, casting a look at Betty, who was smiling from ear to ear.

"Well, good bye for now. Thank you so very much, David. Words cannot describe how we feel at this moment," he said with a catch in his throat.

Betty lowered her head in assent, hiding the tears of relief she was shedding.

After they had left, David smiled at Miranda and said, "Thanks a lot! What a great idea!"

She smiled back at them and said, "We thought so! Bye for now!" as she rose through the ceiling and disappeared once more.

In the meantime and during the drive home, Dan asked, "Well, Honey, what do you think about all of this?"

Betty was bubbling with excitement and exclaimed, "Just think about everything we've seen, heard, and experienced during the last few hours! It's completely mind boggling! Brandon is healed, and we're being offered the chance of a lifetime! It's so wonderful! Aren't you just thrilled? Miranda is magnificent—and I do mean that in every sense of the word! We can learn so much, just as David and his family already have. Even if we learned nothing at all about healing, the ability to travel to another Planet is so exciting!"

He smiled, thinking, "She is completely caught up in the idea already. Her face is glowing with anticipation. Just thinking about all of the endless possibilities is almost too much to contemplate! I can only imagine the changes that we could make in people's lives!"

"It's a lot to think about, indeed," Dan said aloud with a chuckle. "It's truly almost unbelievable, except for what we just witnessed!" he added as an afterthought.

CHAPTER 26

After being released, Bob went to his apartment. When he got there, he sat on the couch, thinking about the whole situation.

He thought, "I'm still angry about having the Restraining Orders served on me by the Desk Sergeant! Here I thought I was going to get off easy when David dropped the charges against me. I know Julie told me she was going to do it, but it was still a dash of cold water in my face when it happened. I had such grand ideas when I came up here! Just look at me now! I've messed up everything! I not only have a son, but a grandson, too. There's a good likelihood that I won't ever be able to see them again! After the way I acted, who could blame any of them? That makes me very sad."

With that thought, he got up and got ready to take a shower so he could get cleaned up.

As he stood there, letting the warm water hit him, he thought about Jonathan and David: "I waited such a long time—all these years—and I thought about what I might say to my son when I did see him. Like an unthinking fool, I reacted poorly, caused by the alcohol. I know I cannot change what's already happened, but somehow I could try to make amends in the future if I can just get my act together!"

Right then and there, he decided: "I'll show them all that I'm not just a drunken jerk! It's important to me that I do whatever it takes to redeem myself! I want to show David, Melody, Jonathan, and Julie that I am indeed a nice person who can be successful, as well as upstanding."

Bob kept this thought uppermost in his mind, using it to goad him on in his efforts to change. He went back to work and performed every task with a determination he did not know he had. Days flowed by and blended into months. His expertise and ability did not go unnoticed by his boss, Sam Knots, who summoned him to his office one day.

Bob walked into the office and found Sam sitting behind a desk covered with building blueprints.

With trepidation and expecting the worst, he asked, "You sent for me, Boss?"

"Oh, yes, grab a chair," Sam responded, motioning with his right hand as he hung up the phone. "I wanted to talk to you a few minutes to get your opinion," he stated. "We're building houses like crazy, and we need to expand—which brings me to you. For some time now, your work has been outstanding. In fact, you've demonstrated to me the knowledge and capability to assume more responsibility. How would you feel about supervising your own crew? Later, if you can handle it, we could add in maybe a second and possibly a third crew. I don't have to tell you that business is booming. We need more skilled carpenters, framers, drywall workers, electricians, plumbers, brick layers—entire crews. Do you think you would be interested in doing that? It would mean a lot of work for you and a lot of extra hours. I would make it worth your while, you know."

Bob's sense of trepidation dissipated as he listened intently. He tried very hard to conceal his excitement.

He thought, "Here it is—my moment—what I've been working so hard for. It's actually paying off!"

Aloud, he said with a big smile, "I could handle that, Boss!"

Sam rose, leaned over the desk with his hand extended, and said, "From today, you can now call me by my first name. I know you can handle the job because, frankly, I've been watching you closely for this last year. I had my doubts when you got put in jail, but you've allayed all my fears. Since then, you've been very dependable and hard working as I could possibly ask for from any man."

Bob said, "Has it been that long? Really?" as he grabbed his hand in a firm handshake.

He laughed and said, "Time flies when you're having fun. We've got to hire more people. You can start by screening these applications and interviewing the workers. We need to hire the best people as quickly as we can while this building boom is humming. There's a lot of money to be made!"

"I'm all for that," said Bob, joining him in the laughter.

"As soon as we're through with the hiring, I'll go over the necessary blueprints and the lists of houses which will take a priority with you. Well, how does it feel to be a boss yourself?" Sam asked.

"It feels just great! I'm really looking forward to this. Thanks for this opportunity, by the way. I appreciate it more than you know," he replied.

"Good!" Sam exclaimed. "I'll see you first thing in the morning so we can get started. We've got a lot of work to do to make all this happen!"

"I agree, but we can do it!" Bob jubilantly replied as he turned to leave.

He left for his apartment. His spirit was soaring.

He said aloud, "I cannot remember a time when I felt this good!"

Then he had a sobering thought, "Well, perhaps there was another occasion—when I married Julie. Well, I cannot change the past—just my future. This is why I've worked so hard. The opportunity I've waited for all my life is happening. I just cannot believe it's been a year already! Tomorrow, when I get to work, one of the things I want to ask Sam is how I can buy one of the houses we are building. I now know that the way I can make money is to buy a house, finish the landscaping, and live in it for a short time. After that, I can put it on the market so I can make a profit. I can even repeat that process. Maybe I could buy two houses as I move upward, renting one and living in the other."

As the months went by, Bob did just precisely that. He worked and supervised his crews daily. Houses went up, and projects were completed either on time or early. His checking and savings accounts grew by leaps and bounds. Business in the building industry kept booming. Because of his expertise and knowledge, his salary moved up handsomely. Bob's investments kept money pouring in, accumulating and compounding. In fact, the months just slipped by, which he barely noticed because he was so busy working and planning.

Two years elapsed. He now had a beautiful home, which he had built with the help of one of his crews. He had personally made changes to the blueprints, modifying, deleting, and adding various rooms and specifications to his own tastes. The end result was a beautiful one-level, ranch-style house. It had a two-car garage and large lawns, both front and back, perfectly landscaped.

Bob was sitting on his couch, thinking, "I've got the world by the tail now. Maybe it's time to give Julie a call and see if she'll join me for dinner and a friendly chat. This time, I'll have to do it right—flowers and the whole romantic show! Who knows, she might even recognize how very much I've changed since I don't drink anymore. The last time I tasted a beer, which was ages ago, it tasted so bad that I had to spit it out! That was it for me! Only good things have happened since then. I hope she'll tell me about David, Melody, and Jonathan."

"Well, here goes," he said aloud as he picked up the phone to dial Julie's number.

A woman's voice answered the phone, "Hello."

"Julie, this is Bob. Please don't hang up. I know I've been a jerk beyond words, but I want you to know that I'm sober. I've been sober since that awful night," he blurted out.

There was silence on the other end of the phone, but she did not hang it up.

She thought, "Is it really him? It doesn't sound like the Bob Michaels I know. He sounds different—more commanding even. I wonder if what Jonathan said can be true—I wonder if he really did cure him of his drinking problem?"

Finally, she asked, "What do you want?"

He responded, "Honestly, I just want to take you out to dinner and talk with you—a real date, you know? It will be public, and I'll bring you home anytime you want to go."

She wondered again, "Is it possible? Could he be cured?"

Aloud, she asked, "Do you promise to behave yourself?"

He thought, "Yes! This could be my chance to repair all the damage I've done."

He answered, "You've got my word on it! How about we do it on Friday night—dinner and possibly a movie—just something casual?"

She paused for a moment and responded slowly, "I think that will be all right. How about six o'clock? I am assuming you have my address."

"You know I do," he answered. "See you then," as he hung up the phone.

He was so elated that he just shouted, "Yes! Yes! Yes!" to the room at large.

He thought, "This may be my only chance with Julie, so I'd better put my best foot forward."

He got out the phone directory to look up a local florist and made a call to order flowers. Afterwards, he went into his walk-in closet to select his clothes, already planning what he was going to say and do.

"This time, I'll do it right!" he promised himself.

CHAPTER 27

Dan and then Betty went to Gorbandihar as planned for their training. Both of them realized immediately how far behind humans were in technology. Dan could not get over the quality of the color televisions and super quiet moving conveyances he saw there. Betty always spoke of the pure intelligence, wisdom, and kindness displayed by He Who Summons and Miranda. The cleanliness and beauty of Gorbandihar stuck in her mind, along with the friendliness of the beings there.

Time passed quickly. Brandon was nine years old now. Both Dan and Betty were doing many healings.

They were in their living room, sitting on the couch talking.

"You know, Honey," he said, "it's ten times easier to heal a person than it is to conceal the fact that you did anything."

She laughed and replied, "Now you know what David has been going through. Many times I've caught myself wondering how he did it and still kept the news media from discovering what he was doing. Anyway, we've been invited over to their house for dinner."

He laughed as he opened the hall closet to retrieve his coat, taking Betty's out as well so he could help her put it on.

"It's wonderful to have this awesome knowledge and power to heal, but it's also a huge responsibility. Think of the tremendous good we could do if we could perform it openly," he said as he helped her into her coat.

She turned and gave him a big kiss and a hug.

"Oh, we've been over this many times before, and nothing has changed," she replied. "If we could do it openly, we would probably be hounded by the news media and even people with imaginary illnesses. Of course, we would in all likelihood be accused of performing Black Magic by scores of uninformed people. No, Darling, I think He Who Summons is right—for now. I agree with Him that our society is just not ready to accept that there are other beings out there that are far more advanced than we are at this time."

She grabbed Brandon's coat as she called him, "Come on, Son. We have to go."

"Where are we going, Mom?" he asked as he came over to her to get his jacket.

She answered, "We've been invited to Jonathan's house for dinner. Oh, and don't forget your pullover cap and gloves—it's really cold outside."

When they were on their way, Dan asked, "Who is going to be over there besides us, Betty?"

"I think maybe Julie, but as far as I know, that's all," she said.

"It will be nice to see them again and catch up on what everyone has been doing," he said, grinning.

"Yes, it will be good," she responded. "They really are wonderful people. We will always be indebted to them for helping us with Brandon."

"Yes, there is that, for sure," he replied soberly in a softened voice.

He thought, "I remember taking our son to the hospital after he was healed to have his blood drawn and tested. Everything came back normal—proof indeed that he was OK. He didn't run a temperature anymore and has been full of vitality and energy ever since. Life has been good, and we are so very grateful for that. We both now realize that happiness does not have anything to do with money or the lack of it. Service to mankind is more rewarding and satisfying. We've been doubly blessed because Betty is with child again!"

He reached over and patted her tummy.

She placed her hand over his and spoke softly, "You know, Dear, because genetic transference occurred from David to Jonathan, it might happen with our child. Have you thought any about that possibility?"

His mouth flew open in amazement as he replied, "No, not at all!"

She laughed, squeezed his hand, and said, "We'll have to stay alert for signs. Did I tell you that the ultrasound shows that it will be a little girl?"

"Really? That's wonderful! Could we name her Christina Elizabeth after our mothers?" he asked excitedly.

She laughed again and replied, "Of course, Darling. What a wonderful idea!"

He pulled up in front of David's home and parked his car. He turned and gave her a great big kiss in celebration of this news. After that, they went up to the porch and rang the door bell.

Melody opened the door, smiled, and said, "Please come on in. Merry Christmas everyone!"

"Merry Christmas!" they responded.

"Here, let me take your coats," said Melody as she took them to hang up.

"Your house is decorated beautifully," said Betty.

"I second that," said Dan.

"Where's Jonathan?" asked Brandon.

Melody laughed and said, "Well, the last time I saw him, he was watching cartoons on television."

Brandon went to look for him.

David came into the hallway, smiled, extended his hand towards Dan, and said, "It's good to see you guys again."

"We are happy to be here with you," replied Dan as he firmly shook David's hand.

"Come on in. Mom's already here," David related, "and we have a lot of catching up to do."

They moved into the living room, and Betty walked over so she could sit down by Julie.

"Merry Christmas," she said, smiling at her.

"Thank you, and a very Merry Christmas to you and your family," she responded.

When everybody was seated, Dan and David immediately launched into a conversation about Gorbandihar.

Betty looked at Julie and asked, "How have you been doing? We don't see one another enough. It's been such a long time."

Julie sighed and answered, "Yes, it has been a long time. I'm still working at Fitzsimons, as you've probably already guessed. I've been Divorced for three years now. A funny thing happened a while back. My ex-husband, Bob, called and wanted to take me out for a date—dinner and a movie—so we could talk. I agreed to go. You cannot imagine how surprised I was when he came up to my door. He'd put on weight and was dressed very nice. He even had a beautiful bouquet of flowers for me!"

David had overheard, so he and Dan stopped talking.

David said, "Are you kidding? What were you thinking, Mom? Don't you still have Restraining Orders against him?"

She replied, "No, I cancelled them because they were not needed any more. He's so very nice. He's doing really well. He's a boss at his company and is running crews that build houses. He's even bought a nice new house that he planned and built himself."

"Well, it sounds good, but what about his drinking problem?" he asked.

"Well, he hasn't had a drink since he got out of jail. He tried a beer once, and it tasted so bitter he had to spit it out," Julie said as she winked at Jonathan.

David laughed loudly.

Jonathan's ears had picked up when he saw Grandma Julie's wink.

Now he stood up and stuck out his chest, "I told you I cured him!" he stated proudly.

"Well, I'll be, Son. Sounds like you did at that. In fact, you had a really good idea," David told him.

Melody went into the kitchen to check on dinner and set the table. She called Jonathan and Brandon, who followed her.

"Why don't you two grab your jackets and play in the back yard for a few minutes until dinner is ready?" she asked. "It's cold outside, but dinner will be ready in about twenty minutes. Would you guys like that?"

Jonathan was already tugging on his coat as he glanced back at Brandon.

He said, "Come on. We can throw my football around."

In the meantime, David looked at his Mom and admonished her, saying, "After all you went through with him, I'm surprised you would even consider such a thing!"

"Well, Davey Boy," she laughed and said, "you may know a great deal about healing a body, but that does not mean you know everything about feelings—and love."

Betty nodded her head in understanding and smiled. Dan was grinning as well. David's face mirrored his confusion as he shook his head from side to side.

Finally, David said, "So what happened?"

"Well," she answered slowly, "we had a wonderful time that night—so extraordinary in fact that we have done it many times since then."

Melody had heard raised voices in the living room and came in to investigate the reason.

"No!" exclaimed David and Melody together, looking at each other with that reserved look in their eyes.

She smiled and said, "Well, I guess there's no time like the present to show you my early Christmas gift."

She held out her left hand, which flashed a beautiful engagement ring.

"But you said that you were done with him!" exclaimed David.

"Yes, you are right. But I've found that I still love the man I married so long ago. I was willing to give him another chance since he seemed so different now. Besides, I trust Jonathan when he said he cured your Dad of his drinking problem. You would be amazed at the man he has become! In fact, I promised him I would tell you all about it. He wants to come over now, but I told him I would have to get your OK first. He's waiting for my call now with your answer."

David then looked at Melody, questioningly.

She nodded her head in assent as she said quietly, "I have to trust Jonathan as well."

David shrugged his shoulders in response and replied, "Mom, you have always known what you want and what is good for you. You can call him and ask him to come over."

She smiled brightly, went over to the phone, picked it up, dialed a number, talked briefly, and came back with an even bigger smile.

She said to the group, "He'll be over shortly."

Julie motioned to Betty and said, "Let's see if we can help Melody set the table and help with dinner."

"Great idea!" Betty said, laughing as she rose to join her.

Soon the table was reset, including a new place for Grandpa Bob. The food was also placed on the table.

Melody went to the back door to call the boys in for dinner when she stopped to witness the little drama unfolding in the back yard. She motioned for both Betty and Julie to come and see, placing her fingers over her lips so they would be quiet. When Betty realized what was happening, she quickly went into the living room and beckoned for Dan and David to come as well. All of them were looking out the back door glass and kitchen windows.

Jonathan was slowly advancing towards a dove that was dragging a wounded wing, moving towards the back privacy fence. There was no telling how the bird got injured. At any rate, the dove was flapping its wings, struggling to fly, but going nowhere. Brandon was on Jonathan's right side, trying to herd the wounded bird towards Jonathan, who was speaking softly to the bird as he slowly advanced. He stopped and extended his hands towards the fluttering bird. Brandon sensed that he should stop and remain motionless as he watched Jonathan. The dove continued frantically flapping its good wing.

Jonathan began slowly moving his hands and felt the heat generating outward towards the injured bird as he concentrated.

He thought, "I've never tried to do this without actually being near whatever I am healing, but this just has to work! That bird is just not going to let me get close enough to do what I normally do!"

Slowly, the dove stopped fluttering and remained perfectly still. Jonathan took a couple of small steps towards the bird and kept sending out warm, healing moves from his hands. The dove now appeared to be unafraid.

Everyone inside the house was watching Jonathan. Melody, Julie, and Betty exhaled loudly, not realizing they had been holding their breath. Melody was smiling, while both Julie and Betty were mesmerized. David and Dan exchanged glances, grinning and nodding their heads in admiration.

A monitor screen on Gorbandihar was lit up. He Who Summons and Miranda were in front of it, watching intently as Jonathan performed his healing on the little bird.

Jonathan very slowly advanced towards the dove, bent over very carefully and softly cupped his hands. The dove stood completely still. Jonathan easily picked up the bird and kissed the top of its little head. He smiled at Brandon. Gently, he opened his hands, giving the dove an upward lift towards the sky.

Snow began falling as the dove flew away, its wing completely healed. They watched as it made a semi-circle and flew back over their heads as if to say, "Thank you."

All the women inside were now smiling as they dabbed at the tears in their eyes with tissue paper.

David had a large lump in his throat, watching his son heal the dove.

He thought: "Amazing! He's only eleven years old! How did Jonathan accomplish that feat? How did he know what to do?"

Meanwhile, on Gorbandihar, He Who Summons turned from the screen and, with a large smile, He beamed at Miranda and said, "Young Jonathan displays an understanding of our advanced healing techniques. Because he is young, his mind is not cluttered with what he cannot do or what may be impossible. Instead, he is willing to explore any possibility. Soon he will be a master. He has great potential, and I am very pleased with his progress. He will do great things, just wait and see!"

She brought Him a glass of elixir and said, "Let's do a human toast." She lifted her glass, clinked it against His, and exclaimed with a smile, "To a brighter future for all humans on Planet Earth!"

He smiled in agreement and stated, "And here's to Christina Elizabeth Hollis. I just can't wait to see the wonders that she will perform!"

Miranda smiled as They sipped Their elixirs, thinking, "I'm certainly looking forward to training her when that time comes!"

Back on Planet Earth, Jonathan and Brandon came running in the back door as Melody called them to dinner. The boys took off their coats and hung them up. Just then, the doorbell rang. Jonathan ran to the front door and opened it.

He yelled, "Grandpa!"

Bob came into the room, sheepishly smiling until he saw Julie. His face lit up like a Christmas tree. She immediately went into his arms, and he gave her a big kiss.

He looked at everyone and said, "Hi! Thanks for inviting me tonight. You don't know how much I appreciate that!"

David walked over, shook his hand, and said, "You are most welcome here. By the way, you clean up really good!"

Bob was embarrassed again and said, "Well, I'm not that man anymore. Thank you for giving me a second chance." He looked into David's eyes and said as he tousled Jonathan's hair, "I just want to learn how to be your Dad—and his Grandpa!"

Jonathan gave him a big hug and said, "You don't need to learn something you already know. It's only about loving and caring."

On Gorbandihar, two Beings laughed and said, "We could not agree more!"

Meanwhile, back on Earth, Jonathan looked at everyone, his eyes shining with delight and satisfaction.

He smiled from ear to ear and said, "This is going to be the best Christmas ever!"

The End

(Or Is It The Beginning?)